Ian Strachan

Ian Strachan was born in Altrincham, Cheshire and now lives with his wife and children on the Staffordshire/Shropshire border. Having worked in the theatre, radio and television, he now concentrates exclusively on writing books for young people of all ages. **Wastelanders** is the sequel to **throwaways**, now a major BBC TV drama series. Both books express some of the deep concern he feels about the way in which children around the world are treated by grown-ups.

Also in the Contents series

Also by Ian Strachan

Contents

WASTELANDERS

IAN STRACHAN

mammoth

This book is especially dedicated to all the people who took the time and trouble to write to me after reading throwaways to say, 'And then?'

The future is not what it was. **Paul Valéry**

First published in Great Britain in 1997 by Mammoth
an imprint of Reed International Books Ltd
Michelin House, 81 Fulham Road, London SW3 6RB
and Auckland, Melbourne, Singapore and Toronto

Copyright © 1997 Ian Strachan

The right of Ian Strachan to be identified as the author
of this work has been asserted by him in accordance with
the Copyright, Designs and Patents Act 1988

ISBN 0 7497 2908 2

10 9 8 7 6 5 4 3 2 1

A CIP catalogue record for this book
is available from the British Library

Typeset by Avon Dataset Ltd, Bidford on Avon, B50 4JH
Printed in Great Britain by Cox & Wyman Ltd, Reading, Berkshire

Extracts from the 21st Century Dictionary

Catchers

Originally used to describe people employed to collect stray dogs, now more commonly refers to officers of the Child Protection Unit (qv) who remove homeless children from the streets.

Child Protection Unit

Groups set up to assist the police with the control of homeless children and supposedly provide welfare for them.

Skulls

Disorganised packs of criminals who roam the countryside, particularly the wastelands. Motorised muggers, usually operating in a variety of unsafe stolen vehicles, who roam around, largely unchecked, robbing or destroying everyone and everything in their way.

throwaways

Children who, for various reasons, no longer form a part of organised society. Though many find some sort of jobs – picking off rubbish tips is popular – many are involved in petty crime and they often roam the streets, where they also sleep.

wastelands

The outcome of the removal of hedges and the widespread use of chemical fertilisers, which made it possible to produce larger crops from smaller amounts of land. To prevent farmers overproducing, and prices falling, governments in rich countries paid farmers to *not* grow crops on large areas of land. This scheme was originally known as 'set-aside'. At first the land was cared for, but as the scheme became widespread, and more and more land lay unused, much of it went to waste. Some reverted to woodland and provided habitat for wildlife or the homeless. But, for the most part, due to the intense use of chemicals in the past and the effects of global warming, huge quantities of dusty prairie land slowly eroded into desert which became frequented by Skulls.

One

'Get down Chip!' Sky shouted, pressing her younger brother's head into the weeds which grew up the sides of the ditch.

As the vehicles rapidly drew closer the noise of their engines increased.

'Are they Skulls?' Chip whispered.

Sky nodded her blonde head.

When they had lived in the city their greatest fear had always been of being picked up by the dreaded Catchers; out in the countryside the gangs of Skulls posed an ever-present threat.

Chip asked, 'Did you see how many of them there were?'

'Two at least, but I didn't stop to look properly.'

The pair held their breath, hoping the Skulls would roar past, but there was a squeal of brakes and the vehicles skidded to a halt immediately above them. Suddenly the clean, country air was tainted by the stench from the idling engines of exhaust fumes and hot oil.

'There were definitely two kids,' a voice insisted above the engine noise. 'Honest, Chains, I saw them.'

'OK, Wheels, so where are they now?' another, huskier voice demanded.

Chip eased his way up the bank and carefully parted the weeds to get a better view. Parked only metres from them were three vehicles; a motocross bike, a battered pick-up truck, from which the cab had been removed, and an old car. The bare-chested biker, Wheels, was dressed solely in black leather flying boots and a pair of greasy black jeans. When he removed his goggles to search the horizon, Wheels exposed the only clean patch of skin between head and waist.

Slumped in the driver's seat of the pick-up truck, her bare feet on the dashboard, was a young girl in a brown tank top and a pair of faded denim cut-offs. Her hard, bony face was made to look even more severe because her head was completely shaved apart from one long, thin strand of hair. Dyed fluorescent pink, it rose from one side of her shiny, bald crown and hung down over one shoulder.

The car was a typical Skulls vehicle which had been stripped down to its basics. The body looked as if the top had been removed by a giant tin-opener. Around the sides, the jagged, rusty edges were bent outwards to dissuade anyone from approaching it. The bonnet and wings had also gone, leaving the engine completely exposed. The bull bars bristled with spotlights and a tubular-steel roll-bar protected the driver's seat. This was occupied by a man of about twenty-five, whose head was also shaved. The black leather waistcoat he wore over his naked upper body was festooned with row upon

2

row of metal chains. The well-defined muscles of his bare, tanned arms were heavily tattooed and smeared with glistening black streaks of engine oil.

'They've got to be around here somewhere,' Biker complained.

'So? Find them!' the other Skull croaked.

Wheels pulled down his goggles, revved his engine and sped off round the field in a cloud of dust. As he left, the girl in the pick-up slowly lit a cigarette.

'You could kill yourself using those, Pinkie,' Chains observed as he hauled himself out to peer into the bowels of his engine.

'Yeah, yeah!' Pinkie drawled.

Wheels eventually returned and reported, 'No sign of them.'

'Why don't you look down there?' Chains asked, nodding towards Sky and Chip's hiding-place. 'Rats and vermin often hide in ditches.'

'Come on!' Sky hissed at Chip. 'Run for it.'

But while the biker was still gingerly easing his way down the steep slope, Chip, with Sky close behind him, was already running and stumbling along the bottom of the ditch.

'I've got them!' Wheels shouted up to his mates. As the moto-cross bike skidded along, its rear wheel sending up a great arc of mud, the vehicles above accelerated to keep pace.

'He's gaining on us,' Sky yelled breathlessly.

Chip called back over his shoulder, 'Keep going.'

But when the water in the bottom of the ditch grew suddenly knee deep, running became impossible. Sky soon found herself stumbling along through sticky mud, which sucked at her feet. As her foot slipped off a stone and sent her sprawling in the smelly water, she yelled, 'Chip!'

Suddenly, the front wheel of the bike was only two metres away from Sky. 'Why don't you give up now?' Wheels scoffed. 'You'll never get away!'

Chip staggered back, scooped up a handful of black, sticky mud and hurled it at the biker. The mud splattered across Wheels's goggles, temporarily blinding him, so that he lost control of his bike. His front wheel ran up the side of the ditch, pitching him off into the water and then, as the bike toppled, its engine spluttered and died.

Wheels scrambled to his feet, hauled his machine back up and began cursing when it wouldn't kick-start.

Chip grabbed Sky's hand and began to drag her forwards. Suddenly, from above, Chains croaked, 'Going somewhere?'

Chip and Sky froze. Looking up, they saw Pinkie and Chains were both standing at the top of the ditch. Pinkie, using an aerosol paint can, was busy spraying the trunk of a tree with their gang sign – a lime-green '&'. Chains leered down at them, ominously tapping the long, glinting blade of a knife against his oily palm.

'Let's get out of here,' Chip muttered as he lurched forward, grabbing Sky's arm and pulling her along.

But, as they struggled through the water and slime, Chains only had to stroll along the bank to keep up with them. 'You might just as well give up now,' he suggested. 'You're annoying me and I'll make you pay for it in the end.'

'He's probably right,' Sky admitted, freeing herself from Chip's grip, 'we'll never get away from them.'

As Chains slowly slithered down the bank, he grinned. 'Now you're talking!'

But Chip, who was now several metres ahead of his sister, called back, 'Sky, keep going! I've found a way out.'

He was standing on a low brick parapet. Ditch-water was flowing over his feet, down a steep concrete overflow and into a river below. 'Quick!'

Feeling as if she was moving in slow motion, Sky fought against the clinging mud, whilst Chains plunged along after her. He was so close she could smell the mixture of engine oil and sweat from his body.

Just as Chains reached out to seize her, Chip grabbed Sky's hand and almost threw her over the ledge. Chip only had time to see a sudden flash, as the Skull's knife-blade whistled past his face, before he launched himself down the overflow, after his sister.

With only the muddy water to lubricate their slide and thin clothing to protect them from its uneven concrete surface, they hurtled uncontrollably down the steep incline. It was a short but painful journey. Sky grazed her elbow and Chip ripped his jeans, skinning both knees, before they fell off the end and plunged beneath the surface of the fast-flowing river.

When Sky eventually surfaced, shaking water from her face, Chains was still standing at the top of the overflow. 'Don't think you've escaped,' he roared down, his husky voice echoing around the wooded valley. 'Next time we meet, I'll finish you both off!'

But at that moment, Sky was more worried about Chip, who could not swim and had yet to surface. She frantically trod water as she looked around her. 'Chip, where are you?'

She was just about to dive back beneath the murky water to look for him, when she heard him calling, 'Sky, I'm over here.'

Downstream of her, Chip, his brown hair plastered to his head, was desperately clinging to an overhanging branch to avoid being swept away by the force of the current.

Sky managed to swim across. She got her arms under his shoulders and eventually they both scrambled up on to the bank, where they collapsed, exhausted.

'That was a close one!' Chip murmured.

When she'd recovered her breath, Sky suggested, 'We'd better get out of these wet things.'

They washed the mud off their torn clothing and hung it out to dry over some bushes. As they lay on their backs in the sun, after the roar of vehicles and the scare of the chase, the sound of birdsong and the steady ripple of water suddenly seemed so peaceful, until Chip complained, 'I'm hungry.'

'Me too,' Sky admitted.

'No, I'm not just hungry,' Chip said, correcting himself, 'I'm starving! I need a couple of hamburgers and a mountain of chips.'

'Oh, shut up! Talking about it only makes it worse. We'll probably find something later on.'

Chip's anxious brown eyes searched her face. 'Will we? How do you know that?'

Sky sighed. 'I don't, not for certain, but we usually manage.'

'All I had to eat yesterday were those two raw potatoes, which we managed to dig up before the farmer's patrol came along, and one green apple.'

'I got exactly the same. I know it's not much, but the end of the summer's always the worst time. Soon there'll be plenty of ripe fruit, berries and nuts.'

But Chip wasn't convinced. 'We can't keep fighting off the birds for food and, anyway, before you know it, it'll be winter again and we'll be back with the same old problem.'

Sky vividly remembered one particular night, the previous winter, which they had spent in the ruins of a fruit-packing shed. Desperately tired, their stomachs aching with hunger, they had huddled together under some damp sacks, in a fruitless attempt to keep warm. They woke next day, their fingers stiff and blue with cold, to find themselves covered by a thin layer of snow which had drifted in through holes in the roof.

'What else can we do?' she asked.

Not for the first time during the last two years, Chip quietly suggested, 'We could always go back to the Tip.'

Sky immediately remembered the stench of the enormous rubbish pile, which they'd lived beside after their parents abandoned them.

Sky would never forget the months they had spent, with the other Pickers, scrambling ankle deep up the huge mound of refuse, searching for the smallest thing which they could either eat or sell. She still had nightmares about the first day they had gone out on to the Tip; she had watched Childie being buried under an avalanche of rubbish. Sky was convinced they would never have survived on the Tip without Dig's help.

'But what about trying to find Dig?' she asked Chip. 'Are we just going to give up?'

It was two years since they'd left the Tip with Spindor, who had given up his job as a Catcher and invited them to join him on a farm he'd bought. Spindor intended to run it as a second chance for some of the Pickers. But, during their journey to Spindor's farm, it had all turned sour. Sky had discovered that Dig, who was supposed to be going with them, had been picked up by Spindor's partner, Shakey. Worse still, Shakey had sold Dig to a farmer. Immediately Sky decided that there was no way she would accept a new life from someone who could just stand by and watch her friend being sold into slavery. It would be like taking blood-money.

From that day forward, Dig had continually been on Sky's conscience. Dig, always wary of anything to do with Catchers, had been suspicious about Spindor from the first time she mentioned him. But Sky had insisted Dig meet him. If she had not, Dig would still be free. Sky and Chip had spent two years wandering around the countryside trying to find him, in the hope that they could rescue him.

Chip had been closer to Dig than anyone, but even he had to admit their search had not been successful. 'We've never found the slightest trace of him. How much longer can we keep going on our own? You saw what happened with the Skulls just now. We were lucky to escape.'

'I don't know why they bother with us. It's not as if we've got anything worth stealing.'

'That's not the point,' Chip countered. 'If they'd caught us they'd kill us anyway.'

'OK, so what do you think we ought to do?'

Chip looked cautiously at Sky. 'Spindor did say, if ever we changed our minds, we could still go and join him.'

'I'd sooner starve to death than take anything from that man,' Sky said bitterly.

'Yes, right!' Chip laughed scornfully. 'So as long as you have a clear conscience, you won't mind a slow, lingering death from starvation?'

'Well, I suppose, when you put it like that . . . but we've wandered around for so long, I've no idea where we are, let alone how to find Spindor's place.'

Chip suddenly raised a finger to his lips to silence Sky.

'Is it the Skulls again?' she hissed.

Chip shook his head and whispered, 'No, it's our supper.'

He was pointing at a rabbit, which was nibbling a patch of grass in a clearing a short distance from them.

Sky put a hand on his arm. 'You can't kill it!'

'Just watch me!' Chip picked up a large round stone. But just as he was taking aim, Sky clapped her hands and the rabbit was gone in a flash.

'Why did you do that?'

'Because I couldn't bear to see you kill that poor little creature.'

'You mean you'd sooner see me die of hunger?'

'No, of course not.'

'Then tell me, what are we going to eat now?'

'We'll find something, Chip.'

'You keep saying that. Like what?' Chip gestured towards the clearing. 'Fancy some grass, or a few leaves?'

'Chip, you're being silly.'

'You're the one that's being stupid. You just lost us a perfectly good meal.'

'We'll find something else,' Sky said calmly and, although they were still damp, she began to pull on her clothes.

'Where are you going?'

'Anywhere,' she said quietly.

'I'm coming with you,' Chip said, reaching for his jeans.

Sky stopped. 'No, I want to be on my own.'

Chip's anger suddenly evaporated as he asked anxiously, in a very small eight-year-old's voice, 'You will come back again, won't you?'

Sky couldn't help smiling. 'Of course I will! I just need some space and time to think, but I promise I won't go far.'

Two

Sky wandered slowly along the riverbank until she came across a large rock hanging out over the water. She climbed on to it, and sat cross-legged, elbows on either knee, her chin resting on her clasped hands, watching the water flow by.

Sky felt guilty about leaving Chip on his own, but lately there were a growing number of times when Sky longed to be alone. Although she was only thirteen, she sometimes felt more like Chip's mother than his sister.

Mother. As Sky no longer had the slightest idea of where their mother was, the very word 'mother' sounded odd and she rarely said it out loud. The only photographs of her Sky owned had long since been lost, along with the rest of their possessions and she could barely remember what her mother looked like.

It was only in her dreams that Mum's image became clearer. A few of Sky's dreams relived the awful moment when she woke in the back seat of their car to find that both her parents had gone. But in the dream, as she awoke with a rising sense of panic, the first thing she saw was the back of her mother's head.

The other recurring dream was set in the kitchen of a house. It wasn't their old one, which they had been forced to leave when Dad was made redundant and the family set off across the country on the long, fruitless job hunt. This was a house she had never seen before and she only knew it was theirs because she recognised some of their old scratched furniture.

When the dream began, though nothing was said, Sky simply knew her father was due home from work any minute. Mum was always busy at the sink, with her back to Sky, preparing vegetables for their evening meal, and when she turned round, Mum always gave Sky a lovely smile.

Whenever Sky felt herself starting to wake, she always desperately tried to hang on to the image of her mother but, somehow, no matter how hard she fought, every time it managed to slip away. Just as Mum had in real life.

Sky never stopped wondering what had happened to her parents. Where *were* they? Had they found work? Most important of all, did either of them ever give a single thought to the two children they had abandoned, asleep on the back seat of that broken-down car?

Sky always blamed her father and drew some slight comfort from her mother's appearances in her dream. That brief, lovely smile seemed to suggest that, wherever she was, Mum had not forgotten them completely and was, in some curious way, still watching over them.

Bearing in mind how casually they were abandoned, Sky found it odd that she should feel such an enormous sense of responsibility for Chip. Life would probably have been easier for her, too, if she hadn't constantly had Chip to look after. But she knew there was no point in thinking like that. Chip was as much a necessity as breathing. Besides, being forced to explain her decisions to Chip had, on more than one occasion, stopped her taking the easy way out when difficult choices needed to be made.

Sky picked up a stone and hurled it into the fast flowing river. This time again, in her heart, she knew Chip was right. They really could not struggle along on their own for much longer. Even if it had only been an excuse, their search for Dig had given their lives some shape and purpose. But the longer the hunt had gone on, without a glimmer of success, the more pointless it had become.

And dangerous too. Lately, there had been a growing number of narrow escapes from the clutches of the Skulls. Soon, their luck might run out.

Sky's thoughts were suddenly shattered by a sharp cry of pain. Was it Chip?

'I knew I should never have left him alone,' Sky muttered guiltily, as she bounded off the rock and ran back. 'I'll never forgive myself if the Skulls have got him!'

Desperate to get back, she forced her way through the undergrowth, ignoring the sharp, clinging brambles which snagged her clothing and tore her bare skin.

'Sky! Help!' Chip's second cry was abruptly cut off and, as

Sky drew closer, she heard sounds of a scuffle.

She burst into the clearing to find Chip lying flat on his back being attacked by what looked like an animal. It was only when she looked more closely that she discovered Chip's attacker was not an animal, but a young boy, slightly smaller than her brother. He had straight, black hair, which hung down almost to the waist and an animal skin partly covered his grubby, but heavily tanned, body. Sitting astride Chip's chest, the boy was raining down blows with both fists.

Protecting himself with his arms, Chip yelled, 'Get him off me.'

Sky, avoiding the boy's flailing fists, grabbed the boy from behind and lifted him away. He immediately twisted round and started trying to claw her face. In the end, she was forced to hold him at arm's length, leaving him harmlessly punching the air, while he snarled ferociously, baring his yellow teeth, like a wild animal.

'Where did he spring from?' Sky asked, still holding on to the fierce creature.

Chip scrambled to his feet, examining his bruised forearms. 'He suddenly leapt out of the bushes.'

Sky shook the struggling boy who, having realised he couldn't reach with his fists, was trying to kick her with his bare feet. 'What *is* your problem?'

Instead of answering, the boy simply redoubled his attempts to attack her.

'Look,' she said quietly, but without letting go of him, 'we haven't done you any harm, so calm down! What's your name?'

Surprised by her complete change of tone, the boy paused for a moment and stared hard into her face. His eyes were almost jet black.

Sky slowly repeated her question. 'What is your name?'

The boy didn't reply, instead he tilted his head slightly on one side, rather like a dog which is puzzled by an unfamiliar sound.

She said again, 'Who are you?'

But the boy only let out a peculiar grunt, more animal than human.

Chip stared in amazement at the boy. 'Sky, he can't talk!' Chip burst out laughing and scornfully prodded the boy with a finger. 'What's up with you, eh? Lost your tongue?'

As the boy twisted and turned, trying to grab Chip's probing finger, Sky snapped, 'Chip, stop that! Leave him alone.'

'He didn't leave me alone – look at these bruises!'

'Maybe he thought you were going to hurt him.'

'He's not so brave now there are two of us,' Chip scoffed.

While Sky was talking to Chip, the boy suddenly wrenched himself free from her grip and, using a stooping, monkey-like run, disappeared into the bushes.

'After him!' Chip cried.

But Sky held her brother back. 'Let him go. He's obviously scared silly.'

'Suppose he's not alone? Maybe he's gone off to find his friends and they'll all come back to attack us.'

'No, I think he is alone,' Sky said thoughtfully. 'In fact, I rather think he's always been alone.'

Chip was stunned by the idea. 'You mean for ever and ever?'

'Well, he must have had a mother,' Sky agreed. There was that word again! 'But perhaps she died while he was still a baby, or maybe she just left him out here in the woods. I suppose he could have been brought up by animals, like Romulus and Remus.'

'Who were they?'

'Twin boys who were supposed to have lived thousands of years ago in Italy. As babies, they were left in the country to die, but a she-wolf found them and she brought them up as if they were her own wolf cubs.'

Chip liked that idea. 'I'll call him Wolf Boy.'

'Not being around humans might explain why he doesn't talk,' Sky suggested.

'And did you see the way he ran,' Chip grinned, 'almost on all fours?'

'Oh, well, I don't suppose you'll have to call him anything now he's gone.' Sky looked around her. 'Are we going to stay here, or move on? Because if we're going to stay, we ought to think about finding something to eat and maybe light a fire. My clothes still aren't properly dry.'

'I suppose we could stay here, as long as Wolf Boy doesn't come back.'

'I think you're right, he probably won't risk taking on both of us. I'll start gathering some firewood.'

Chip produced a soggy box of matches. 'We'll need some dry grass first. The matches got soaked while we were in the river.'

'Have you still got your bottle end?'

Chip nodded and, from his other jeans pocket, he pulled out the round, polished base from a milk bottle, which he'd picked up years ago on the beach near the Tip.

'Then we'd better be quick and get it lit before the sun gets any weaker,' Sky urged.

As there had been no rain for some weeks, it was not difficult to find fuel. They swiftly made a pile out of dry grass, bracken, leaves and small twigs. To avoid the fire spreading they built it on bare earth and surrounded it with stones. Chip used his bottle end as a magnifying glass. By tilting it slightly, he managed to focus the sun's rays into a bright pinpoint of light and after several false starts, the dry material charred, smouldered and eventually burst into a tiny flame. With her face at ground level, Sky blew gently into the centre of the smouldering heap, while Chip carefully added more twigs.

By the time the sun had dropped out of sight behind the steep shoulder of the river valley, they had a good fire going.

'I only wish we had something to cook over it,' Chip moaned. 'Do you remember that time we were in town with Dig and he asked us where we'd like to eat – Pizza Hut, McDonalds or Kentucky Fried Chicken?'

Although the joke had been on her, Sky laughed. 'I thought he must have sold some wonderful piece of scrap and was using the money to buy us a real meal.'

'But all he meant was, which litter bin did we want to search first!' Chip grinned, but quickly grew more serious. 'Sky, we're never going to find Dig now, are we?'

Sky picked up a stick and stirred up the fire. Reluctantly she agreed. 'Probably not. I mean, we can still keep a lookout for him, but I think you're right and we ought to make proper plans, so that we don't have to struggle through another winter.'

'So, what's it to be?'

Sky's stick suddenly burst into flame and she quickly dropped it into the centre of the fire. 'Maybe we ought to try and find Spindor. Just to see how he's getting on after all this time. It's not as if we have to commit ourselves. We can say we've only come on a visit and then, if we don't like what we see, we can always leave again.'

'What if we hate it, but he won't let us go?'

Sky shot a worried glance at her brother. 'Why wouldn't he?'

Chip shrugged. 'Well, he was a Catcher.'

'Yes, but he's not one any more.'

'I suppose you're right, but it seems to me that what Dig said is true; one way or another, people always let you down.'

'Chip, I promise we'll be very careful. Anyway, we've got to find Spindor's place first. Maybe tomorrow we should stick to this riverbank. I remember there was a river close to his farm. Mind you, it wasn't nearly as big as this one, we easily crossed the ford in his pick-up truck.'

'In that case, maybe we ought to walk upstream, towards the source.'

Sky nodded. 'OK. Now, shall we gather some more wood to keep the fire going? It would be nice not to have to go to sleep in the dark for a change.'

As they got up, Chip grabbed Sky's arm. 'Look, there's somebody lurking in the bushes. I think Wolf Boy's back.'

Sky called out to the boy, 'We've seen you, so you might as well come out.'

But instead of showing himself, the Wolf Boy bombarded them with a hail of stones, bits of wood and anything else he could lay his hands on.

Chip was about to retaliate until Sky stopped him. 'Leave it!'

'Are you mad?' he asked, dodging an incoming missile.

'If we throw stuff back, it'll just turn into an all-out war. But if we don't, he might give up. After all, we are on his territory and he probably doesn't understand we want to be friends.'

'Friends!' Chip yelped, as a lump of wood struck him a painful blow on the ankle. 'He's got a funny way of showing it.'

But as soon as he realised they had no intention of striking back, Wolf Boy parted the bushes and cautiously walked towards them. Hanging from his hand, by its ankles, was a dead rabbit.

'Sky, look, after all that, he's brought us a present!'

But the boy ignored them both and walked, wide-eyed, towards the embers of their fire, which were glowing red in the dark. Before they could stop him, Wolf Boy touched the hot ashes with his bare foot. Letting out an agonised cry, the boy leapt back and then began punishing the fire for hurting him, by beating it with the rabbit.

Chip stopped him. 'It's OK, the fire won't hurt you if you keep your distance.'

Warily watching the fire, as if it might attack him again at any minute, Wolf Boy solemnly offered Chip the dead animal.

Chip thanked him but, holding up the limp rabbit, its fur bedraggled with a mixture of blood and ash, he turned to Sky and asked, 'What am I supposed to do with this?'

'You wanted to kill the one we saw earlier,' Sky said scornfully. 'I thought you knew what to do with it. We certainly can't eat it like that.'

Seeing their hesitation, the boy grabbed the rabbit back. He took a sharp-edged flint stone from a pouch in the hide he wore and skilfully began to skin and gut the creature.

The sight and smell of the rabbit's innards was too much for Sky. She offered to collect wood to rebuild the fire. But, by the time she returned with an armful of twigs and branches, Wolf Boy was already sitting cross-legged, a safe distance from the fire, using his yellow teeth to rip the tough, raw meat from a leg bone.

Sky, whose stomach hadn't properly recovered from the smells of the guts, said in disgust, 'How can he do that?'

'It doesn't look easy,' Chip observed. 'Shall we cook ours over the fire?'

Wolf Boy, the half-eaten leg poised in the air, watched in open-mouthed amazement as Chip and Sky quickly put together a wooden frame to go over the fire. But when Chip thrust a stick through the centre of the carcase and prepared to roast it over the fire, Wolf Boy dropped his meat in his hurry to stop them wasting good food.

Fending him off, Chip tried to explain, 'I'm only going to cook it.'

But Wolf Boy still looked annoyed and moaned unhappily, as if Chip was spoiling his precious gift.

'It'll be all right,' Chip promised him.

In spite of Chip's assurances, Wolf Boy made several more attempts to rescue the rabbit. In the end, Sky handed Wolf Boy the raw leg and forced him to sit down and watch.

During the whole time the rabbit was cooking, the boy never looked away from the fire. When the sap in a piece of wood overheated, making it go off with a loud crack, Wolf Boy jumped up in alarm and headed for the bushes again. It was quite a while before he decided it was safe to return.

Eventually Chip's impatience got the better of him. 'Do you think it's cooked yet?'

'It smells all right,' Sky admitted. Even Wolf Boy's nose had started twitching and sniffing like a dog's. 'Let's try it.'

Chip found his knife, which was an exact replica of the one Dig had originally made for him from the end off a tin can. Gripping the taped handle, Chip used the serrated edge to hack off a piece of meat. He handed it to Sky, 'Try it.'

'Mmmm!' Sky, unable to remember when she had last eaten a hot meal, moaned with sheer pleasure. 'It's delicious!'

Chip sawed off the three remaining legs and handed them round. Wolf Boy ignored his and instead reached out for Chip's knife. 'Mind you don't cut yourself, it's very sharp.'

But Wolf Boy was obviously used to learning by watching. At the first attempt, carefully holding it by the handle, the way Chip had,

Wolf Boy cut himself a sliver of meat. Delighted by his success, Wolf Boy grinned at Chip.

'Now try eating the meat,' Chip urged, waving the leg in Wolf Boy's face.

Because the bone was still hot, the boy held it very gingerly, sniffing suspiciously at the meat. Seeing how much the other two were enjoying theirs, he took a small experimental bite but, being unused to cooked food, he immediately spat it out and blew between his lips to cool them.

Sky and Chip couldn't help laughing, a sound which Wolf Boy seemed to enjoy. He joined in and laughed louder than either of the others.

When he eventually got his first proper taste of the cooked meat, Wolf Boy looked as if he'd been poisoned. However, he soon realised, now the meat was cooked, it was much easier to eat. Even so, Sky noticed, the moment he'd finished the roast leg, Wolf Boy quickly went back to gnawing the familiar flavour of his old, raw bone.

Three

Next day, Sky woke from an uneasy sleep to find Chip shaking her. He was looking rather disappointed. 'Wolf Boy's gone.'

'Don't worry, we'll manage. We did before we met him.'

'Not all that well,' Chip pointed out.

Sky rubbed her stomach. 'I think I must have eaten too much yesterday. I'm not used to having proper food and I kept waking all night with stomach-ache.'

Chip grinned. 'Me too! Wasn't it great?'

'I'm still so full, I don't think I'll need to eat again for days.'

As Sky was speaking, the bushes behind them parted to reveal Wolf Boy. He walked towards them holding something in his cupped hands.

Sky, who had still not recovered from the last lot of innards, asked hesitantly, 'What's he brought this time?'

'Eggs! He's brought us five eggs,' Chip said, holding up one of the olive-green eggs.

'They may be the same size,' Sky observed, 'but they're definitely not hen's eggs.'

'I don't care if they're snake's eggs,' Chip declared. 'I'll eat them anyway.'

Sky shook her head. 'I don't know how you can find the room after last night's huge meal. Mind you,' she added, 'it's years since I had a boiled egg. If only we had something we could use as a saucepan.'

'He's got a better idea,' Chip said.

Wolf Boy used a stick to poke a hole through the shell and then put the egg to his mouth and sucked, very hard. After the first mouthful he grinned, smacked his lips and wiped a stray trace of egg yolk from his chin.

Sky shuddered. 'How can he do that? I could never eat them raw!'

But Chip was willing to try anything once. 'It's not so bad,' he announced. 'A bit slimy, but really quite nice.'

'But what about the mother bird, when she goes back and finds her nest's been robbed?'

Chip thought she was using that as an excuse. 'I bet you'd eat the eggs if we could boil them.' He was proved right later in the day when he found an old tin can down by the river in which to boil the water.

Over the next few days, to Chip's enormous delight, Wolf Boy tagged along with them while they slowly travelled upstream. At first Sky was worried about taking the boy away from the territory he knew best. 'He might not be able to survive in a strange place.'

But either Wolf Boy easily adapted to new surroundings, or he had travelled far more widely than Sky thought. On more than one occasion, when Chip and Sky believed they had found the best possible camp site for the night, Wolf Boy insisted on going further and they ended up in a better place. Once he took them directly to a dry, well-hidden cave.

That particular night Chip greatly amused Wolf Boy by drawing matchstick people on the smooth parts of the wall with charcoal from the fire.

Certainly, wherever they took him, Wolf Boy had no difficulty in finding things for them to eat, and he took great pride in sharing his knowledge of hunting and foraging with Chip.

Sky, who had never seen so much blood, was often forced to cover her ears to try and block out the heartbreaking cries of dying animals and birds. Fortunately, for Sky was beginning to wish she could turn vegetarian, Wolf Boy also knew a great deal about wild plants. He showed them which leaves were safe to eat and sometimes pulled up plants and made it clear that the roots were the best part.

In return, when Chip found some tangled line with a hook on the end, left behind by a careless angler, he wanted to show Wolf Boy how to fish.

'I can just about remember going fishing with Dad once,' Chip said to the boy. 'We'll have to wait until we can find some bait.'

Chip and Sky always talked to Wolf Boy, though from his reactions it was obvious he did not understand a word, and he usually replied with a variety of grunts.

He called them both something which sounded roughly like Sky. This had started when Sky tried to tell him who she was by pointing at herself and repeating her name over and over again. Wolf Boy grinned and imitated her.

Sky was very pleased with her instant success, until he pointed to himself and again said, 'Skiee.'

She'd tried to explain, but he was too excited by the sound he was making to listen and, from then on, he had used the same word for almost everything except, as Chip pointed out, the blue space around the sun.

But, when it came to practical things, Wolf Boy was undoubtedly a quick learner, though occasional mix-ups occurred.

While Chip was looking for bait, he came across the remains of a huge ant-hill built out of pine needles. It must have been knocked over by an animal searching for food. Thousands of ants were frantically trying to repair the damage, which had exposed the white larvae in their nest.

'Sky, give me the can so I can collect some.'

'We've got to drink out of that!' she protested.

But Chip took it anyway. 'Don't fuss! We can always wash it out with boiled water.'

Chip plunged his hand into the nest and grabbed a handful. When Wolf Boy saw what Chip was doing, he thought Chip was collecting the grubs to eat. He scooped up a handful, which he crammed into his mouth, ants and all.

'Don't eat them, they're for fishing!' Chip said, but Wolf Boy was munching away quite happily, occasionally spitting out the odd ant.

It was Wolf Boy's turn to look puzzled when they returned to the riverbank and Chip baited the fish hook with a grub. When Chip cast the line out into the river, Wolf Boy burst out laughing.

'What's up with him?' Chip asked.

Sky helpfully suggested, 'Maybe he can't understand why you want to drown perfectly innocent grubs. Come to that, neither can I.'

'You won't laugh when I catch us a nice big fish,' Chip muttered defensively.

Sky grinned. 'More a case of, if, rather than when!'

For some time they sat in a silent line along the bank. Occasionally Wolf Boy dipped into the can and, as if he were taking sweets or crisps, ate another grub.

'Maybe he's got the right idea after all,' Sky observed. 'He's probably getting more nourishment out of those grubs than we will if you don't catch something soon.'

Chip did get as far as picking up a grub and rolling it between his fingers, but in the end he couldn't bring himself to eat it.

Bored, Sky lay back in the sun and asked lazily, 'What are we going to do with Wolf Boy if we manage to find Spindor?'

'What do you mean?'

'It's all very well letting him come with us – and he's taught us a great deal about living off the land – but, don't forget, Wolf Boy's probably never seen a house, let alone lived in one.'

'Maybe Spindor will let him camp out in the garden or something.'

Sky frowned. 'Remember how choosy Spindor was about who he'd take with him?'

'Yes, especially when it came to Dig,' Chip murmured bitterly. 'But we can't just run off and leave Wolf Boy. Anyway, he's so good at tracking, he'd easily find us again.'

Sky suddenly sat up, sharply alert. 'Did you hear something just then?'

Chip listened. 'What sort of thing?'

'I thought I could hear engines, way off in the distance.'

Chip listened again and then shook his head. 'I can't hear anything.'

'I keep thinking the Skulls have come back to look for us. Must be my imagination,' Sky said.

She looked at the two boys, sitting side by side. Chip's back covered by his tattered shirt and Wolf Boy, naked and deeply tanned. Wolf Boy had grown bored with the fishing and was busy sharpening spears. Maybe, she thought, if Spindor allowed Wolf Boy to stay with them, then Chip might start to get over missing Dig so much.

Her eye traced Wolf Boy's dark, tangled mane of hair as it hung over the brown velvet of his skin. She watched the movement of his slim, strong wrists as he worked and guiltily wondered, was it only for Chip's sake that she hoped Spindor would allow Wolf Boy to stay with them?

Spending every day with her brother was all very well, but, just lately, Sky had found herself wondering about boys. Thinking back to when she was at school, most of her mates already had boyfriends and by now they were probably going steady together. But the weird lifestyle she had been thrown into, which was in many ways so free and intimate, had made Sky very wary of forming close personal relationships. Even so, Sky couldn't help wondering what a real kiss would be like.

Sky's thoughts were rudely interrupted by Chip giving her a violent dig in the ribs, as he cried out, triumphantly, 'I've got a bite.'

When he hauled out the fish, which was far larger than anything Wolf Boy had been able to spear in the shallows, Chip was really pleased with himself. Although it was only mid-afternoon, he couldn't wait to taste his catch. 'Let's cook it now!'

Sky looked worried. 'Is that such a good idea?' They normally never lit fires during the day in case someone spotted the smoke.

'Just this once,' Chip pleaded.

They collected grass and wood for the fire, and Chip offered Wolf Boy the piece of glass. 'Why don't you light it?'

But the boy shrank away from Chip's outstretched hand. Although he would sit, at a very safe distance, from the fire, Wolf Boy had resisted all attempts to teach him how to light one. If either of them lifted out a burning piece of wood, the boy would rush off and hide in the undergrowth. It was as if he believed that fire was not only potentially dangerous, but unnatural, possibly bad magic.

When the fish was cooked and eaten together with some leaves and roots Wolf Boy had collected, it made a delicious meal.

Sky licked her fingers clean. 'That was a beautiful fish, Chip.'

'It was good, wasn't it?'

'I tell you,' she sighed, 'I haven't felt this full since the night Wolf Boy brought us the rabbit.'

Chip grinned happily. 'Are you sure we need to bother finding Spindor? I could quite happily live out here with Wolf Boy for the rest of my life.'

'Maybe you're right,' Sky agreed.

'Kind of you to send up the smoke-signals and let us know exactly where to find you.' The harsh voice of Chains suddenly sliced through their contentment.

Sky and Chip spun round to find the shaven-headed Skull, standing behind them. With Chains, apart from Pinkie and Wheels, were seven or eight other equally evil-looking Skulls.

Chip yelled, 'Run for it, Sky!'

They both leapt up and raced through the trees, the Skulls letting out loud whoops as they gave chase. But Sky and Chip had hardly gone any distance before they were captured.

'Leave me alone!' Chip protested, squirming and kicking as he tried to free himself from the grip of a red-faced boy, whose pale head was shaved to leave a coxcomb of ginger hair.

'Don't you harm my brother!' Sky warned.

'Or what?' demanded a tall Skull with greasy, black, shoulder-length hair.

'Or you'll be sorry,' Sky said lamely.

The Skull shook his greasy locks mockingly. 'Oh, Mum! Help me! I'm so scared!'

He picked Sky up by the waistband at the back of her jeans,

threw her up and caught her under one arm. Ignoring her thrashing arms and legs, he carried Sky back and dropped her unceremoniously on the ground, knocking all the wind out of her.

'Where's the other one?' Wheels asked.

The redhead looked around. 'What other one?'

'The one that looked like a dog.'

Having recovered her breath, Sky was about to pick herself up off the ground when a large boot came down painfully between her shoulder blades. The boot's owner growled, 'I'll tell you when to move!'

'Never mind,' Chains said, 'these were the two I really wanted. The two who gave me the grief.'

Pinkie sidled up to him and asked, in a bored voice, 'So, now you've caught them, what are you going to do with them?'

'I'll decide that when I'm good and ready,' Chains growled. 'But first we search them. I don't want to leave here empty-handed.' He rounded on Chip and, towering over him, demanded, 'Turn out your pockets.'

'I haven't got anything,' Chip muttered.

'I said, turn out your pockets!'

Reluctantly, Chip obeyed. In front of the Skull, he dropped some orange baling twine, the fishing-line, his knife and the piece of glass they had used for lighting the fire which had given them away.

'And the rest!' Chains demanded.

Chip hung his head. 'There isn't anything else.'

'Yes, there is! I can see the shape of something against your jeans.'

'It's nothing,' Chip said sulkily. 'Nothing you'd want anyway.'

'Give it here!'

From her position, still pinned to the ground by the boot, Sky was only able to raise her head slightly. She was amazed to see Chip produce a tiny, blue, toy pick-up truck, the only thing Chip had taken with him the day they left their car. It was Chip's very last link with their old life. Sky had not seen the toy truck since they were at the Tip and thought he had lost it ages ago.

'What's this?' Chains scoffed.

Chip hastily closed his hand round the toy truck and tried to stuff it back in his pocket, mumbling, 'I told you it was nothing you'd want.'

But the Skull grabbed Chip's wrist. He thrust his face close to Chip's and snarled, 'Why does everyone keep trying to make up my mind for me? Drop it!'

Chip kept his fist tightly shut. 'I said, it's just . . .'

'And I said, DROP IT!' Chains shook Chip's wrist and, when that failed, squeezed it hard, digging his thumb viciously into the soft area around Chip's pulse.

With a cry of pain, Chip dropped to his knees. As he did, the toy fell from his hand. Chip lurched forward to grab it, but Chains was too quick for him and jammed his boot down on top of the car.

'Give it back!' Chip yelled. 'It's mine.'

'Not any more it isn't, kid!' Chains quickly lifted his boot and then brought it down heavily, crushing the car between his sole and the rock it rested on, grinding his heel until there was nothing left but a shapeless bit of metal.

Sky expected Chip to go mad, but he got up and stood in sullen silence in front of the Skull, his head bowed.

'Well, that was a whole heap of fun!' Pinkie said tartly. 'Now what?'

The Skull grabbed hold of the girl's face and twisted his hand until he had forced her to her knees. 'We're going to have a party.'

Silently, the girl pulled away from Chains. She got up, took out her paint spray can and began putting their lime-green territorial mark on the surrounding tree trunks.

'You've had your fun,' Sky grunted, 'why don't you just let us go?'

But Chains shook his head. 'Don't leave now – the fun's only just beginning! You three, tie them to those two trees with the kid's baling twine. The rest of you can go and get the beer from the cars. Then we'll all sit round the campfire they kindly built for us and have us a party.'

'You don't need us here for that,' Sky grumbled while she was dragged off to the tree, where the greasy Skull forced her bare arms back painfully against the rough bark and tied her up.

'Oh, but we do. You're my guests of honour. The whole reason for having the party. Remember the promise I made you, last time we met, when you ran off? Well, the high point of this party is when I make good that promise and kill you both.'

Sky flinched as Chains demonstrated the method of killing he intended to use, by drawing an oily forefinger across his throat.

Four

The echoes of the Skulls' party rang out through the woods for several hours, during which time a great deal of beer was drunk. Long after dark, they were still dancing and swaying around the fire, climbing trees and breaking off branches to keep it alight. Arguments frequently broke out, several turning into fights, with the losers usually ending up in the river. But, eventually, as more Skulls fell into a drunken sleep, the fire slowly died down to a dull red glow and an uneasy silence descended, only broken by sleepy snorts and grunts.

After sitting on the ground for hours with her arms stretched out behind her round the tree, Sky was stiff and uncomfortable. She waited patiently until she was convinced it was completely safe, then whispered through the darkness, 'Chip, are you all right?'

'Yes, I'm OK, but what about you?'

While the Skulls were at their liveliest, they had taken pleasure in competing with each other to find different ways of humiliating their prisoners. These ranged from the childish, like tipping beer over them, to near torture. One of the Skulls got a real kick from using his cigarette end to scorch the hairs off Sky's forearm.

'I'm a bit uncomfortable, but OK otherwise. They're animals!'

'Sky, do you really think they're going to kill us?'

Sky, who had already been menacingly scratched with the point of a hunting knife, had little doubt. 'I'm only surprised they haven't done it already.'

'What are we going to do?' Chip asked.

'I can hardly move. How can I *do* anything.'

'I know. I've been trying to twist my hands round to see if I can get at the knots, but it's hopeless. I can't get anywhere near them.'

After a short silence, Sky murmured, 'It's a bit stupid to say this when we could both be dead by morning, but I'm so sorry they smashed up your car. I know how much it meant to you.'

When Chip replied, his voice wobbled slightly and Sky knew he was trying not to cry. 'I always meant to throw it away anyway. I don't really know why I've hung on to it all this time.'

Sky changed the subject. 'I'm glad Wolf Boy got away. I think they would have been very cruel to him.'

'This doesn't exactly feel like a day at the beach!' Chip scoffed.

The next time Sky spoke, Chip didn't answer and she thought he must be asleep. She would have loved to escape from this nightmare into sleep, but instead she sat in the dark, listening to the unpleasant noises of the sleeping Skulls and the friendlier sound of the owls hooting to each other in the branches above her head.

For the first time for ages, Sky found herself wishing she knew what time it was. Ever since they had moved on to the Tip she had slowly lost all track of time. Years, dates and months had become meaningless. She only recognised the changing seasons by the weather and the amount of food available. For the rest, it was pointless to know if it was somebody's birthday, or three o'clock. Surviving until the next day, whatever it was called, was all that really mattered.

But now, probably because she was aware she had very little left, time suddenly seemed terribly important. Soon after daybreak, when the Skulls woke, she would almost certainly be dead.

How long was it to sunrise? How long was it since the Skulls turned up? Were there only hours, or was most of the night still left? Was the brightness she could see in the distance coming from a low moon, or was it the first glimmer of daylight? Daybreak usually felt so welcome, but this one could be the last she ever saw.

The phrase ' . . . the condemned prisoner's last meal . . .' flashed into her mind and she was pleased hers had been the fish Chip caught. That suddenly struck her as funny. She began to mutter, over and over, 'Chip's fish! Fish and Chips!' The more she said it, the funnier it sounded and she began to giggle hysterically, but then the giggles slowly broke down into sobs.

Seconds later, a hand clamped firmly over her mouth.

A voice whispered in her ear, 'Skiee.'

Wolf Boy had come back! He immediately began cutting at the plastic baling twine but, with only his sharpened flint, it seemed to take ages. Sky was terrified someone would wake before she was free. Several times, against the dull glow of the fire, she saw the vague outline of limbs stirring as someone rolled over in their sleep.

After what seemed like hours, her hands were free. She struggled stiffly to her feet, gently rubbing the feeling back into her legs and chafed wrists.

Wolf Boy's shadow flitted across to Chip. He put his hand over Chip's mouth, but Chip woke with such a start that Wolf Boy lost his balance and there was a sharp crack of dry twigs as he fell backwards.

Sky desperately wanted to take off and run as far as possible from the Skulls, but she knew she had to wait for the others.

When nobody stirred around the camp fire, she crept over to Chip. He hissed impatiently at her, 'This is taking for ever! Why don't you see if you can find out what the Skulls have done with my knife?'

Sky whispered back, 'It's not worth the risk of treading on somebody's hand in the dark. Hang on, it won't be much longer now.'

Just as Chip was finally free and he was getting to his feet, a voice suddenly yelled out, 'What's going on over there?'

'Let's go!' Sky hissed, and she grabbed Chip's hand so that they wouldn't lose each other in the dark.

'I can't!' Chip howled. 'I've been sitting for so long, I've got pins and needles in my foot.'

'Wake up!' the Skull shouted. 'Them kids are getting away.'

Even as Sky threw Chip's arm over her shoulder and, half carrying him, began to run, she could hear people scrambling up. When she glanced back, looking for Wolf Boy, Sky saw that some of the Skulls were lighting hastily improvised torches in the embers of the fire.

The feeling slowly returned to Chip's foot, and they plunged blindly through the undergrowth.

The Skulls' shouts and cries echoed eerily through the dark wood. But soon they were drowned by the angry growl of motocross engines joining in the chase, their headlight beams flashing across the treetrunks. Whenever they caught sight of the fleeing figures there were renewed cries of, 'There they are! This way.'

Fortunately the Skulls were slowed down by the after-effects of all the beer. Those on foot kept tripping over and falling to the ground where they lay rolling about, laughing drunkenly. And, although the bikes provided better light, they kept colliding with trees and each other, pitching their riders into the undergrowth.

Sky, still trying to force a path through low branches, looked back to see if the Skulls were gaining on them. As she did, she suddenly lost her hold on Chip's hand. The ground gave way beneath her and she started to fall.

She let out a series of half-stifled yelps of pain, as she plummeted down the steep bank, catching in patches of brambles and bumping against saplings.

Chip, fumbling his way forward, tried to follow his sister more cautiously, but even he slid part of the way and got a nasty blow on the head from an overhead branch.

When he finally managed to reach the bottom, he stumbled about in the pitch dark with outstretched hands, trying to locate Sky by her low moans. Eventually he found her arm. Hearing her sobs, he anxiously asked, 'Sky, what's the matter?'

'It's my leg!' she moaned. 'During the fall I caught it on a rock.'

'Do you think it's broken?'

Between sobs she murmured, 'I don't know, but it feels as if it's been sliced in half.'

Very gently, Chip felt for her injury. One leg of her jeans had been ripped open. She gave a sharp intake of breath when he touched the wound, which felt sticky.

'Leave it!' she said sharply.

'I was only trying to find out if there was a bone sticking out.'

'Just leave it alone!' Sky hissed at him.

'Can you get up?'

'I'm not even going to try.'

'But what about the Skulls?'

'Shut up a minute!'

They listened and realised that the noise of the Skulls was fading away into the distance.

Chip said, 'I think they've lost us.'

'In that case we might just as well stay put until we can see where we're going. I doubt if they'll ever come looking down here, and that way we won't fall down any more ravines in the dark.'

Chip wondered, 'What do you think happened to Wolf Boy?'

'I don't know. I didn't see him again after we left the camp, but we've got him to thank for still being alive,' Sky said firmly and then yelped with pain when she accidentally moved her injured leg.

'Is there anything I can do?'

'No,' Sky said wearily. 'I just want to sleep. It's probably shock, but we both need the rest. There's no knowing what'll happen to us tomorrow.'

'Maybe Wolf Boy will just turn up with breakfast as usual.'

'In one way, I hope he doesn't,' Sky murmured.

'Why not?'

'Think about it, Chip! I know Wolf Boy's a better tracker, but if he can find us, so can the Skulls. Anyway, he's probably realised we're the ones the Skulls are after and he's better off without us.'

'True.'

'Now let's try and get some sleep,' she said.

Chip listened to the shuffling noises she was making, trying to get comfortable amongst the leaves, before he whispered, 'Sky.'

'What now?' she snapped.

'I don't really like the idea of you sleeping over there on your own,' he said quietly. 'Anything might happen to you and I'd never know.'

Sky could hardly keep the smile from showing in her voice as she asked, 'So?'

'Maybe you'd feel safer if you held my hand,' he suggested.

And maybe you would too, she thought, but she said, 'Yes, I would, as long as you come on the other side, well away from my injured leg.'

Very carefully, Chip used his hands to find out exactly where she was. He stepped over her and curled up close beside her. But with so much to think about, it was difficult for them to get to sleep and the birds were already chattering in the branches above them before they eventually drifted off.

*   *   *

'It looks awful, all that blood and stuff,' Chip said, impressed by Sky's gaping wound, which ran from half way down her thigh to well below the knee.

'Thanks, Chip! That makes me feel much better!'

'Sorry!'

It was still quite early in the morning and they were examining Sky's leg by the slightly eerie light which filtered down to them through a canopy of leaves. They had woken to find that they were lying at the bottom of a deep ravine and it was hardly surprising the Skulls hadn't found them. Apart from the occasional broken twig, there was almost no sign of their route down. Most of the trees and bushes must have immediately sprung back into position the moment they had passed.

'If we were still by the river,' Sky muttered, as she carefully picked out bits of grass and stone from the gash, 'I could wash out more of this dirt.'

'I'll fetch you some water if you like, Sky.'

'I don't want you going anywhere without me. Besides, what would you collect water in?'

Chip looked glum. 'Oh, yes, I'd forgotten we'd lost the can, along with Wolf Boy and everything else.'

'Forget it, Chip. The things are gone and that's all there is to it. Come on! We can't hang about here for ever. Give me a hand to get up. I want to see how well I can walk with this leg.'

Putting most of her weight on Chip, Sky, her teeth clenched to stop herself from crying out, slowly hauled herself upright and took a few faltering steps.

But it was obvious to Chip that she was suffering. 'How does it feel?'

'Not good. But I'm probably only a little stiff from lying still all night.'

Chip turned away and sniffed. 'Can you smell burning?'

Sky sampled the air. 'Yes, I can.'

'You don't think Wolf Boy's still around, do you?' Chip asked hopefully.

Sky shook her head. 'He was always terrified of fire. It's either the Skulls, or somebody else.'

'I'd better climb up and take a look.'

'Take care,' Sky cautioned.

As Chip struggled up the steep face of the ravine, the smell of burning wood grew stronger with every step. Wisps of smoke blew overhead and unusual numbers of birds, crows and woodpigeons, flew past.

By the time he reached the top, the smoke had thickened and he could easily see the source – the wood was ablaze.

With no rain for weeks, sheets of yellow, crackling flame were rapidly sweeping forward, consuming the tinder dry undergrowth. The heat had grown so intense that even leaves on the trees ahead of the main fire were shrivelling up and bursting into flame.

Chip hastily slithered and skidded his way back down to Sky. 'We've got to get out right now! The whole wood's on fire and it's heading this way.'

As Sky slowly heaved herself to her feet, she muttered bitterly, 'I bet it was started by those crazy Skulls and their flaming torches!'

'Maybe we'll be safer if we go down towards the river.'

With Sky leaning heavily on him, they set off. Their progress was much slower than the fire's. Several times they were overwhelmed by clouds of hot, black smoke, only to emerge coughing, spluttering and rubbing their sore eyes. Apart from the smell of smoke, their nostrils were also filled with the acrid smell of singed hair, caused by the red-hot fragments of ash which were raining down on their heads.

Chip kept anxiously glancing over his shoulder and struggled to stay calm as he said, 'It's still gaining on us.'

'I'm sorry, but I can't go any faster.'

Eventually they arrived on the riverbank, but with the fire right behind them, Sky was not sure they had done the right thing. 'Now what? What with fire on one side and the river on the other, we're completely cut off.'

'I suppose we could jump in the river,' Chip said, looking doubtfully at the swirling water.

'But you can't swim and, with this bad leg, I'm not sure I'd have the strength to keep us both afloat.'

'Look! Isn't that a bridge?'

Half-hidden by a bend in the river, Sky could just make out the grey stonework. 'We'll never make it.'

'We've no choice. Come on! We can paddle down there along the edge of the river.'

They stumbled through the muddy water, urged on by the fire, which was keeping pace with them along the bank. Dodging burning branches which fell, hissing, into the river, they managed to keep themselves cool by occasionally dipping their heads below the surface.

By the time they were level with the bridge and had crawled up the bank, the fire had formed a tight, hungry circle around them. The heat from it was almost overwhelming and only their soaked clothing saved them from being burned.

Once across the bridge, and a safe distance from the fire, they sank down in the grass to watch it rage past them. They could hear the distant bray of sirens as fire engines began to arrive on the far side of the wood.

Some time later, they were still looking out across the desolate scene. In the vast panorama of smouldering, charred remains, only the occasional blackened tree-stump broke up the monotonous grey landscape.

Maybe it was because of the throbbing ache in her leg, but Sky could not help feeling that the scene before her, where familiar objects had all the colour taken out of them, until they became mere shadows, represented the current state of her own life. While other people appeared to live in full-colour, she only existed in a black-and-white sketch.

'What a terrible waste!' she observed.

Chip, always the more practical, said, 'I only hope Wolf Boy got out safely.'

'But what will he do now – that was his home?'

'Yes, I know, but, just at the moment,' Chip said, glancing down at Sky's injured leg, 'I rate Wolf Boy's chances of survival much higher than ours.'

Five

'You really need a doctor,' Chip said, looking anxiously at his sister, who was limping along beside him.

They had had been travelling upstream for four days and, although they saw nothing of the Skulls, they froze every time they heard the sound of an engine. As Sky's leg got rapidly more painful, they had made very slow progress, even after Chip had broken a slim branch out of the hedge for her to use as a walking stick. She had been forced to use unboiled river water to bathe the wound and Chip had sacrificed several strips of material from his shirt to use as bandages. But the gash had failed to heal and rapidly became infected. Flies buzzed endlessly around the pus which oozed from the weeping wound. Sky was also flushed and sweating from a high temperature.

They were halfway up a hill, which overlooked a rocky landscape, broken only by the occasional stunted tree. Sky could not help smiling. 'I don't think we're likely to find a doctor out here.'

'Does this look anything like the countryside around Spindor's?' Chip asked hopefully.

Sky wearily shook her head. 'Not remotely, I'm afraid, Chip. Spindor must live beside a completely different river.'

'I suppose we ought to keep moving.'

'I'm sorry, Chip, but I can't go on for now. I need to rest.' Stiffly, and with a grunt of pain, Sky lowered herself to the ground.

Sky's periods of rest were growing more frequent and, every time they stopped, Chip worried that she might not be able to get up again. The main reason for wanting to press on was the hope that they might meet somebody who could help her.

Food was also becoming a problem again. As they slowly climbed out of the main valley, the broad, flowing river had rapidly reduced to a rocky stream. Though they had clear water to drink, there were no fish, even if they'd had the means of catching them. There was less wildlife, too, and they were forced to manage on the few leaves and roots they could find. With every day they were becoming increasingly hungry and weak.

'I promise I'll feel better after a minute or two,' Sky tried to assure him, but soon afterwards she lay back against a clump of purple-flowered heather and closed her eyes.

Chip patiently waited until his sister was asleep before he quietly left and carried on up the hill to survey the landscape. If they were nowhere near Spindor's and there was nothing else there, Chip could see little point in trudging up to the summit. They would be better off retracing their steps and heading back downstream, where at least there would be more food.

The walk to the top took longer than he expected. Every time he thought he had reached the summit, he discovered yet another rise awaiting him further up the track.

A cool breeze greeted him as he finally reached the summit. Shielding his eyes against the sun, Chip gazed around the desolate landscape. To his left, heather and moorland stretched to the horizon. Ahead of him, after some distance, the moor dropped away into a green valley, which at least offered a distant hope of food.

But it was the totally unexpected sound of a human voice which made Chip turn to his right and blink at what he saw.

The plateau of heather dropped away sharply, until it was halted by a dry-stone wall. The ground beyond the wall grew coarse, dark grass, and eventually rose gently into a round hill, like a shallow, upturned bowl. On the top, in the centre, stood an old tree and, beneath its dead branches, Chip could see a lone figure. Whoever it was appeared to be dressed in something long and white and seemed to be singing and dancing.

Chip wondered if hunger was making him see things? But, imagination or not, Chip let out a relieved yell and waved his arms, to attract attention. Worried that the person might disappear Chip set off at a run, leaping over the tufts of heather. It was easy to find footholds in the limestone wall and soon he was racing across the springy grass.

As Chip drew closer he could see the figure was that of a girl. She had dead-straight, jet-black hair, which hung almost to her waist and flew outwards during the turns of her barefooted dance. The long, white dress made her look very tall and slim but, having such a pale complexion, it was difficult to tell where the material ended and her skin began.

When Chip reached the bottom of the hillock and was close enough to get a good look at her, he was startled to see that the right side of her face was disfigured by a web of thin purple scars, like the veins on a leaf.

The girl was so absorbed in her performance, she was totally unaware of being watched. Her endless song was wordless; just note after note, sung in time with her movements.

Not wanting to scare her, Chip gently called out, 'Hello!'

The girl gave a surprised cry and darted behind the broad, dark tree-trunk.

'I'm not going to hurt you,' Chip said, hoping to reassure her, though she stayed behind the tree.

As Chip walked slowly up the hill, something shiny in one of the branches caught his eye. Although the branches were leafless, they were festooned with decorations. Hanging by threads, in a cross between a mobile and a Christmas tree, were the most astonishing selection of objects.

What had first caught Chip's eye was a piece of mirror reflecting the sun's rays as it turned. Suspended from the wizened branches were countless strips of different coloured tinfoil. Amongst them were hung bits of jewellery, several pieces of broken cutlery and even the handle off an old teapot, with a curved piece of its willow-patterned side still attached. As the breeze stirred the objects, some of them tinkled together like tiny bells.

Though it was a strange, slightly eerie scene to discover in the middle of nowhere, Chip thought it was one of the most beautiful things he'd ever seen. 'I like your tree,' he said loudly.

One dark, serious eye on the perfect side of her face peered out from behind the trunk. 'It's my tree of life,' she said. Chip guessed she was probably around fourteen but, for someone so tall, she had a surprisingly small and high-pitched voice and spoke very slowly.

Having had more time to look around, Chip realised the ground beneath the tree was covered with more of her possessions, mainly in brightly coloured plastic carrier bags. There was also a dilapidated shopping trolley.

'My name is Chip.'

'They call me Gentle.'

'I'm sorry to interrupt whatever it was you were doing, Gentle, but my sister is very ill and she needs help.'

Without replying, the girl continued her one-eyed stare at Chip.

'Do you understand? She's hurt her leg and the wound's badly infected.'

Gentle's mind drifted away into her own past and she recalled, 'I hurt my leg once.'

'Look, could you please help?'

Ignoring him, Gentle continued, 'I hurt it jumping out of a window. See.' She came out from behind the tree and pulled up the hem of her dress to reveal a white thigh covered with the long tentacles of more purple scars.

Chip's curiosity got the better of him. 'How could you do so much damage to yourself by jumping out of a window?'

'It was all the glass. When I jumped I didn't know there was any glass.'

'You mean the window was closed?'

As Gentle nodded slowly, Chip's hopes of persuading the girl to help rapidly began to fade. She was the strangest person he had ever met. He decided to have one last try. 'Look, I'm sorry to bother you and I know it's a bit unlikely, but do you have any idea where I might find a doctor?'

The mention of a doctor seemed to make Gentle nervous. She did not reply and searched about her.

'OK,' he said in desperation, 'just tell me, how far is it to the nearest town?'

After giving the matter a good deal of thought, she replied, 'I don't know.'

Chip was so disappointed and frustrated by the answer, he could have hit her! 'This is hopeless,' he cried. He had been away much longer than he'd intended and was worried what Sky might think if she woke to find him gone. He started back across the field.

'Wait for me!' the girl called after him.

'But I've got to get back to Sky.'

The girl bent down and, from amongst the many bags which surrounded the tree, she picked up a hessian shoulder bag. Round the top it was decorated with tassels and there were bits of embroidery on the sides. As she ran after Chip, she called out, 'I can mend things, all kinds of things. You'd be surprised by what I can do.'

Yes, I probably would, Chip thought. He waited for her to catch up. At the very least, Gentle might be able to help him carry Sky somewhere for help. Though, looking at Gentle's slender frame, he was forced to admit even that seemed unlikely.

By the time Chip got back, Sky was in a bad way. She was lying on her back and, although her eyes were closed, her arms and legs were thrashing about in the heather. She kept shouting out unintelligible words, as if she was trying to fight off the attack of some invisible being.

Chip was very upset by what he saw, but Gentle calmly knelt down beside Sky, glanced at the grubby bandage on her leg and then, placing a hand on Sky's sweaty forehead, announced, 'Your sister has a fever.'

Gentle opened her bag and, to Chip's astonishment, took out a jar of pale green liquid.

'What's that?' Chip asked, grabbing the jar.

'It's just a potion I made up from herbs I gathered. It will ease the fever.'

Chip remembered, in their days on the Tip, Berry's delicious Special Brew. That was also made from herbs. The difference was, Chip had complete faith in Berry, whereas Gentle, to put it politely, hardly seemed to be part of the real world.

'Are you sure that's safe?'

Gentle smiled, apparently amused by his doubts. 'Of course. Besides, do you have any better suggestions? Your sister is very sick and urgently needs treatment. The poison from her injury has got into the bloodstream. That's the cause of the fever. But, if you're worried, I can let her suffer.'

'No,' Chip said uncertainly. 'As long as you're sure you know what you are doing.'

As she took the jar back, Gentle's fingers touched Chip's and he couldn't help noticing, on such a warm afternoon, how cold they were.

Having removed the jar's lid, she took a narrow plastic tube from her bag, and dipped it into the green liquid. She sucked some up into the tube and then placed a finger over the end. 'Please, lift your sister's head.'

Chip did as he was told and watched in disbelief as Gentle carefully put the end of the tube into Sky's mouth and slowly blew the contents down her throat. Sky coughed slightly, but there didn't appear to be any other immediate ill-effects.

Next Gentle caught hold of Sky's twitching, injured leg and cautiously removed the bandage. Having examined the unpleasant wound, she smeared it with a pink paste. Next, Gentle casually walked down the track, plucked some broad leaves from the verge and returned to put them over the wound. 'That should start to draw out the poison,' she said, binding the leaves in place with a strip of blue ribbon from her bag.

Sky had already calmed down a little, but Chip couldn't help wondering if this was just a coincidence.

Gentle displayed no sign of doubt. 'We'll have to wait for a little while now, before I give her another dose of the potion.'

As they sat either side of Sky, with Gentle smoothing Sky's brow with her long, cool fingers, Chip asked, 'Where did you learn about medicine?'

Gentle looked vague. 'I don't remember learning about it. I seem to have always known about such things.'

'Maybe your mother taught you,' Chip suggested.

'I never had a mother and father,' Gentle stated calmly. Then she suddenly said, 'Do you know, at the hospital, they didn't believe I knew anything about medicine and they wouldn't let me help to treat the patients.'

With growing concern, Chip enquired, 'What hospital was that?'

'The one I lived in, of course.'

Chip's eyes opened wide. 'You *lived* in a hospital?'

'Oh, yes! For a long time. I thought everybody did. You see, I couldn't remember being on the outside.'

Chip continued to stare at her. 'Outside?'

'Why do you keep repeating everything I say? *This*,' she said, waving her long, slim arms around her. 'The outside. In the end they made me come out. I didn't want to leave all my friends behind, but they made me. We were split up and all sent to different places.'

'Why were you in the hospital?'

'Because it was my home.'

'But what were you suffering from?'

Gentle looked completely blank. 'Nothing at all. That's probably why they made me leave.'

Chip looked anxiously at Sky, but she seemed to be resting more peacefully and looked less flushed. Even so, he couldn't help feeling guilty about letting somebody, who had been in a hospital, give her weird potions.

'Well, thanks for all your help,' he said briskly, 'but I expect you've got things to do.'

'Not really,' Gentle said dreamily. 'Anyway, I'll have to keep changing the leg dressing and she'll soon need some more of the medicine to keep down the fever.'

'You could leave the stuff with me and I could do it.'

Gentle grabbed her bag and clutched it to her chest, saying sharply, 'No! You can't have my things. They're mine and you shan't take them away.'

Chip hastily drew back. 'It's OK! I don't want to steal anything from you. I just thought, I could give Sky the treatment and then you'd be free to go.'

'But I don't have anywhere to go.'

'What about the place where we met, near your tree of life?'

'But Sky isn't ready to go there yet. I'd far rather stay with you both and help make her better, if that's all right with you,' she pleaded.

Chip was uncomfortable with Gentle but he was even less happy with the idea of being left to cope alone and so, reluctantly, he agreed. 'OK, you can stay.'

Six

'Dad!' Sky yelled in her dream, as she struggled to pursue her father through hordes of Skulls, each one reaching out trying to grab her.

With great difficulty, Chip and Gentle had managed to get Sky back to Gentle's tree, where she lay for the next two days. During the height of her fever, while she lapsed in and out of consciousness, Sky's imagination had run riot through a whole series of wild, exaggerated mind games. These ranged from coming across Dig's dead and mutilated corpse, to walking bouncily across the tops of pink-and-white fluffy clouds, which slowly turned into sticky lumps of marshmallow.

Meeting her parents was a frequent theme, only this time, just as her mother was about to explain why she had deserted them, a strange girl got in the way. She had a scarred face and was dressed in white. She leant in front of Sky's mother, saying something idiotic, like, 'You really should drink more water.'

By the time Sky had frantically thrust the girl aside, her mother had disappeared.

Gentle took Sky's confused behaviour for granted and patiently continued with the treatment.

Sky eventually emerged from the fever. She was completely thrown when she found herself gazing up at the sky through the decorated branches of Gentle's tree of life. The sight of so many everyday objects suspended in midair, backed by fluffy, white clouds, gave Sky the uneasy feeling that she too was drifting in space, or perhaps back in her dream. 'What's happened to me and why are all these things floating around?'

Chip tried to reassure her, 'It's all right. This is Gentle's place. She decorated the tree and she's also been treating your illness.'

Sky still looked confused. 'What illness?'

Chip explained, 'The poison from your leg got into your bloodstream and made you very ill. You've been out of it for the last couple of days, talking to yourself most of the time.'

'You're making it up!' Sky insisted.

Suddenly the girl from her dream appeared, carrying a bunch of leaves. Sky drew back and became quite agitated. 'Get away from me. Don't touch me!'

Chip tried to explain, 'Sky, it's all right. This is Gentle and all she wants to do is change the dressing on your leg.'

'No, she can't touch it, it's too painful!'

Gentle calmly said, 'I think you'll find your injury is much better than when you last looked at it.'

Sky looked down in disgust at her leaf-covered leg. 'What is all this stuff?'

'Gentle put the leaves over your wound to draw out the poison.'

Sky could not believe what Chip was saying. 'Oh, yeah?'

Gentle calmly suggested, 'If you don't want me to touch it, perhaps you should take off the dressing yourself.'

Bewildered by this strange, topsy-turvy world in which people seemed to think it perfectly normal to hang weird things in trees and wrap people's legs up in leaves, Sky carefully removed the strange dressing. She was amazed by what she saw. Although the gash was still slightly inflamed, there was no sign of the yellowy-green pus which had been seeping from it. In fact, a scab was already starting to form. 'I don't believe it!' Sky gasped.

'Neither did I,' Chip confessed. But, for the time being, he decided to keep his reservations about Gentle to himself. The more time he had spent with her, the more certain he had become that Gentle was not remotely like other people. She still sang and danced several times a day. She told him it was her form of meditation, but he found it rather spooky. Aside from all that, he had slowly been convinced that Gentle was well named. She was not only harmless, but also very kind, and she obviously knew a great deal about herbal remedies. Even so, it was an enormous relief for him to see Sky conscious again.

'How are you feeling?'

'A bit groggy.'

'Probably because you haven't eaten for so long. Have some

soup,' Gentle suggested, handing her a plastic mug. Sky looked doubtfully at the thick green liquid and Gentle added, 'It's only potato soup with chopped sorrel leaves to give it a bit more flavour.'

During the next few days, Sky slowly recovered her strength with potions which Gentle brewed from a wide selection of plants, including stinging nettles, comfrey, dandelions and cow-parsley. Gentle used some of these ingredients raw. Others she cooked and several she bottled, adding them to the collection in her bag. She hung bunches of plants in the tree, amongst the ornaments, before crushing and storing the wind-dried leaves for later use.

Although, for the most part, Gentle appeared to be perfectly happy and contented, her life was as sharply divided and contrasted as her face. A simple word, or action, would often trigger another muddled memory from the time she had spent in the hospital.

It was after Gentle had slipped into another of these phases that Sky said, 'I still don't understand why you jumped through the window. Were you trying to escape?'

Innocently, Gentle replied, 'Oh, no. I wanted to be able to fly, like Wings. He told me how to do it, so I tried.'

'Did you ever actually see Wings flying?' Chip asked.

Gentle gave him a pitying look. 'Of course not. He was nocturnal, like an owl. He slept all day and only flew at night. I couldn't possibly see him in the dark, could I?'

Sky was amazed that Gentle, who was so knowledgeable about so many things, could be so easily taken in by Wings. 'And yet you still tried it yourself?'

'Of course. Don't you think soaring through the air like a bird must be the most wonderful feeling?'

'But you forgot to open the window.'

Gentle said vaguely, 'It was a big window on the third floor. If the glass hadn't got in the way, I'm sure I would have flown.'

Sky considered this and then asked, 'Why did you finally leave the hospital?'

Gentle looked sad. 'One day a man arrived with a briefcase. He had all our names in his briefcase and he said that meant we had to leave.'

'Had to?'

Gentle slowly nodded. 'Yes, he said the hospital cost too much to run and they were going to close it down. So we were all sent away to live in different places.'

'Where did you go?' Chip enquired.

'It was a very strange place. The man called it a flat, but when we got there it wasn't flat, it was very tall.'

'You mean a block of flats?' Sky suggested.

'I've just told you,' Gentle insisted irritably. 'There were lots of other people living there, apart from us. A man used to help look after us and he gave us tablets to take, but I hid mine and flushed them down the loo.'

'Why don't you still live there?'

Gentle frowned, struggling to remember. 'I was there for quite a while. But, one day, I went out and couldn't find my way back. Some children started to chase me and I ran and ran to get away from them. Soon there weren't any houses and I was back in the country.'

Sky grabbed at this shred of information. 'You used to live in the country before you went into the hospital?'

Gentle's face clouded over. 'I don't really remember.' Without another word, she strolled off to gather more herbs.

Sky, sadly, watched her go. 'I don't think Gentle ought to be out here alone.'

'She's got us.'

'She has now, but what about the medicine she's supposed to take?'

Chip was not convinced. 'She's managed without anyone until we came along. Most of the time she seems perfectly happy as she is.'

'Most of the time, yes,' Sky agreed, 'but you've seen how quickly her moods change. Suppose she decided to have another try at flying, shinned up this tree and jumped off? Who'd look after her then?'

The only thing Sky and Chip could agree on was that trying to understand Gentle felt as difficult as trying to hold water in bare hands.

By the time Sky's leg had healed, Gentle already sensed their time together was coming to an end. One day she said, 'You'll soon be on your travels again.'

Sky, thinking this might be a lucky guess, said, 'Why do you say that?'

'Sometimes,' Gentle said mysteriously, 'I just *know* these things.'

Late the following afternoon, a heavily built man with a coarse, weather-tanned face came striding towards them across the grass. Over one arm he carried a shotgun, while his other beefy hand gripped lengths of plastic-covered clothes-line which had been slipped through the collars of a pair of snarling mongrels.

'I want you lot off my land by tomorrow,' he announced, then added, looking at Gentle's tree, 'and you're to take all your rubbish with you.'

Sky and Chip didn't much like the look of the farmer, or his dogs, but Gentle was terrified. She cringed away, never taking her eyes off the snapping, slavering jaws of the two dogs.

'Have I made myself clear?' the farmer demanded.

'Yes, very,' Sky replied quietly.

Nodding his head towards Gentle, he said, 'It was bad enough when there was only 'er up here, but it's like I said to my wife, you let one get away with it and before you know where you are there'll be a whole herd of them up there. Then, you two turned up. Next thing we know, there'll be Skulls up here. Anyway, I'm putting sheep on this field tomorrow and I want you gone.'

'We won't harm your sheep,' Chip said.

The farmer pointed at Gentle's possessions, strewn beneath the tree. 'And what happens when the sheep start nibbling at them plastic bags and choke to death? Besides, there's strange things been happening round here ever since she turned up.'

Sky looked puzzled. 'What sort of things?'

'My hens have stopped laying and two ewes gave birth to weird lambs,' the farmer replied.

'What sort of "weird"?' Chip asked.

'One was born with no back legs and the other had a great hole in its skull with a thin skin over it. You could see the poor little thing's brains through it.'

'Wow!' Chip murmured.

'But what's all that got to do with Gentle?' Sky demanded.

The farmer pointed a large, red finger at Gentle, 'She put the evil eye on them.'

Sky gasped. 'Evil eye?'

'Aye! She's a witch!' the farmer declared. 'Everyone round here says so.'

'Surely you don't believe that sort of rubbish?'

'Then why is she always going round picking plants and stuff, if it isn't to put them in her spells?'

Sky laughed. 'She makes herbal remedies.'

'Call them what you like,' the farmer bellowed, 'but if you're not gone by tomorrow, I'll loose the dogs on you.'

Gentle let out a stifled cry and Sky tried to comfort Gentle by placing a hand on her shoulder. 'Can't you see you're frightening her?'

But the farmer was unmoved. 'She'd no right to come here in the first place.'

'She had nowhere else to go,' Chip said defiantly.

'That's not my problem.'

Sky couldn't stop herself asking, 'Haven't you got children of your own?'

'I have, but I'd sooner shoot them with my own gun than let them turn out like you lot – roaming the country and helping yourselves to anything you fancy.'

'We don't enjoy living like this,' Chip snapped angrily.

'We don't have any choice,' Sky pointed out. 'Our parents dumped us.'

'That's no excuse for wandering round the country, stealing and begging from honest, hard-working people like me. Worse, when you've taken what you want, you move on, leaving your rubbish behind you, for others to clear up. Well, I've put up with it for long enough. I'm not having that witch, or you two, living on my land. So, either you clear off of your own accord or, first thing tomorrow, I'll be up here to *make* you go!'

'You ought to be more careful what you say to Gentle, if you truly believe she's a witch,' Sky pointed out. 'Otherwise she might cast a spell over you.'

Without a reply, the farmer turned and stomped off down the hill with his dogs. But, long after he'd gone, Gentle was still shivering with fear.

'It's all right,' Sky said, trying to calm her, 'the dogs have gone.'

'I hate it when dogs shout at me,' Gentle said miserably.

Sky apologised, 'I'm sorry you've got to go. Perhaps we shouldn't have stayed so long.'

Gentle quietly shook her head. 'It's not your fault. Sooner or later, it would have happened anyway. You heard what he said, he thinks I'm a witch.'

'That's superstitious nonsense!' Sky said scathingly.

A tired smile appeared on Gentle's face. 'It isn't the first time I've been called by that name. Anyway, it's probably time I moved on.'

'Where to?' Chip asked.

Gentle shrugged. 'One place is as good as another. If they don't grow crops, or use weedkiller, there are always plenty of wild plants around.'

They helped Gentle gather up her belongings. Chip was up in the tree, carefully putting Gentle's decorations into a bag he had slung over one arm. He called down to Sky, 'I suppose we ought to keep on looking for Spindor.'

On hearing the name, Gentle repeated it. 'Spindor?'

Chip's eyes brightened. 'Do you know him?'

'I'm sure I've heard that name.'

'Please, try to remember,' Sky urged. 'It's very important to us.'

'I just remember another farm and a man . . .' Gentle said vaguely.

'Was he tall, or short?' Chip asked, shinning down the tree. 'Did he wear sunglasses all the time?'

Gentle nodded. 'Yes, he hid his eyes.'

'Were there any young people living on the farm with him?' Chip asked.

Gentle hesitantly said, 'Yes, I think so.'

'But do you remember where this farm was?' Sky asked.

Gentle thought hard, but finally admitted, 'I've lived in so many different places in such a short time and there have been so many people. I'm sorry, I can't remember.'

Sky let out a deep sigh. 'Never mind. I expect we'll find him again one day. Maybe, in the next town we come to, we could go into a library and look at a map.' She reached up to unhook a picture-frame from the branch above her head and was surprised to find it still contained a photograph. Though the sun had faded most of the colour from the picture, it was easy to see the woman bore a strong resemblance to Gentle. 'Is this your mother?'

Taking the frame from Sky, Gentle said, 'Yes.' Tears started to stream down both cheeks. Those running down the right side of her face traced the web of her scars and left them glistening.

Sky hugged her. 'I'm so sorry. We've been talking about what we're going to do, without thinking about your plans.'

'I don't have any,' Gentle sniffed.

'But if you've got a mother, why don't you go home?' Sky asked.

Gentle violently shook her head. 'Oh, no! I can't ever do that! It was my mother who took me to the hospital. She used to say I wasn't right in the head and she wouldn't have me in the house.'

'But that was a long time ago. She might have changed her mind by now,' Sky said. 'Didn't the hospital ask her, when you all had to leave?'

'Yes, but she said she never wanted to see me again.'

'Are you sure? Look, why don't we take you home? I'm sure if she could see you now, she'd feel differently.'

Gentle's sobbing deepened, as she stammered, 'But I don't know where that place is either.'

Chip asked, 'Not even its name?'

Gentle again shook her head. She raised her tear-stained face. 'I was only a little girl when my mother took me to the hospital.'

'Then why don't we go to the hospital?' Sky suggested. 'They must still have your address in their records.'

'But it isn't there any more.'

Sky thought Gentle must be rambling. 'A building can't just disappear.'

'They knocked it down to build a new road. I can never go home again.' Wiping her face dry with the hem of her dress, she suddenly sprang up. 'Come on, we've still got a lot to do and I don't want to be here when those horrible dogs come back.'

Because Gentle insisted that nothing was left behind, even bundles of partially dried leaves, it was dusk by the time everything was put away and the carrier bags piled high in the shopping trolley.

Taking a last look round, Gentle murmured wistfully, 'I did like it here.'

They set off into the twilight, with Sky and Chip struggling to steer the overloaded trolley across the rough ground.

Seven

'Isn't that absolutely beautiful?' Sky sighed.

She was looking down a steep slope towards a huge, oval lake. Apart from the bright orange and red sails of two dinghies, the entire surface was untroubled and reflected the pure blue sky. The lake was set in a broad, lush, wooded valley with only occasional pink or red roofs peeping out from amongst the trees. 'Gentle would have loved this.'

After two days of slow travel, when they were in the middle of a patch of waste ground, Gentle took the fact that the wheel had come off her shopping trolley as an omen and decided to go no further. 'Anyway, I want to stay here, but you two must go on and find your friends.' Reluctantly, they had left her decorating the fir tree in the centre of her new camp which was sited on the edge of a small plantation.

On a particularly hot day, Sky and Chip had found themselves crossing a bleak, arid plain, and they had been tempted to turn back and rejoin her. Even more so when they saw a cloud of dust rising ahead of them, kicked up by another bunch of Skulls crossing their path.

It was late afternoon by the time they spotted the lake. They were glad they had not turned back.

'The moment we reach that lake,' Sky declared, 'I'm going straight in for a swim. I'm so dry, I feel as if, any minute, my skin will crack and I'll crumble away to dust.'

'I wish I could swim,' Chip mumbled.

'If we camp out here for a couple of days, I could teach you. Come on!'

And they ran down the hill towards the water. They were surprised to discover that, just where the landscape abruptly changed from dust to lush grass and trees, there was a high chain-link fence blocking their path. Along the top, hanging out above them, were stretched lengths of razor-wire. Working their way along the fence, they were lucky enough to find a gap, just large enough for them both to squeeze through, and soon they were splashing about in the cool, clear water.

At first, while Sky swam about, diving underneath the water, Chip stayed in the shallows, but Sky remembered her promise and returned to collect him. 'Hold on to my hands and let yourself float,' she said, towing him out into slightly deeper water. 'Stretch out your legs. That's it. Now, kick!'

Chip did as he was told, but lost his grip on Sky and immediately disappeared beneath the surface. When he eventually surfaced again, coughing and spluttering, Chip accused Sky of letting go.

'It's all right,' Sky said. 'That happens all the time when you first start. You just have to keep trying. I promise I won't let anything bad happen to you.'

While Chip was still struggling to stay afloat, the dinghy with the red sail tacked close by. When Sky waved, neither of the people on board waved back, or even smiled.

'Not very friendly!' Sky observed and then suddenly realised Chip had once more disappeared under water. By the time she'd hauled him back up, the boat was gone, beating its way towards the opposite shore.

Chip was just starting to get the idea of floating, when the buzz of an engine caught their attention. 'I hope they're more friendly than that lot in the dinghy,' Sky commented.

'I hope so too,' Chip agreed, 'because that boat's heading straight for us!'

By the time the engine slowed down, only metres from them, they could see it was crewed by two men in uniform, complete with official-looking peaked caps.

'You don't think they're Catchers, do you?' Chip asked.

Sky burst out laughing. 'Out here? On a lake? You've got to be joking!'

But, as the boat nosed into shallower water, above the noise of the idling engine, the larger of the two men barked out, 'Stay exactly where you are!'

Sky smiled at the two men. 'It's all right, we're only having a swim.'

Neither of the men smiled back, or bothered to reply, but the moment they were alongside, they bent over the side and tried to grab Sky and Chip. When Sky moved back out of his reach, the younger man said, 'We don't want any trouble. Just climb into the boat.'

In a flurry of water, Sky and Chip began to wade towards the shore, but the big man shouted, 'Halt, or I fire!'

Sky swung round. To her astonishment, the man was aiming an automatic pistol at them. 'You've got to be kidding! Right?'

The man didn't reply. He merely aimed slightly to Sky's left and squeezed the trigger. As the bullet hit the water, Sky's squeal of surprise was almost lost in the echoes of the gunshot.

'Still think I'm kidding?' The man grinned briefly and then snapped, 'Next time I won't aim to miss. Now, get in the boat!'

'We've only got our underwear on,' Sky protested. 'Our clothes are on the bank.'

'The shore patrol will pick them up. Climb in.'

As they were being hauled over the side of the boat like two wet sacks, Sky noticed a four-wheel-drive vehicle arrive at the water's edge. On its side, painted in large yellow letters, were the words Happy Valley Security. The uniformed driver was picking up their clothing.

As the boat headed back across the lake, Sky said, 'This seems a lot of fuss to make about a swim in a lake.'

Without bothering to look at her, the big man replied, 'The people living round here spent a good deal of money to get away from the likes of you. Didn't you see the big fence they've had put up?'

71

'We thought that was just to keep stray animals out,' Chip muttered through chattering teeth.

'It was,' the big man agreed, 'including you!'

'Everyone ought to be able to use the countryside,' Sky grumbled. 'Lakes and hills ought to belong to the public.'

'This whole area, inside the fence, is a private estate. A few years back this was just wasteland, like the hills beyond. The lake belongs to the people who paid to create it and we're here to see it stays that way,' the man said firmly.

'What happens to us now?' Sky asked.

The man spat over the side of the boat. 'If I had my way, you'd be shot like the rabbits and any other vermin we find in the woods.'

The younger man, who was steering the boat, said, 'We take down your details, return your stuff and turn you out of the main gate.'

Sky was very relieved. 'So you won't hand us over to the Catchers?'

The big man scowled. 'More trouble than it's worth getting them to come all the way out here. But don't get any funny ideas about sneaking back in again because, if I'm alone when I next find you, I won't think twice about getting rid of you for good.'

As the boat pulled in alongside the concrete jetty, one of the dinghy's crew was waiting for them. A tall, thin man, he was wearing a vividly coloured shirt, long, baggy shorts and rope-soled canvas shoes. 'I see you've caught them then.'

The big security guard suddenly seemed to shrink, as he almost saluted the man. 'Yes, sir.'

72

'Well, that's something,' the sailor drawled. 'But I have no doubt they crawled in through the gap in the fence, which I brought to your attention yesterday.'

'Yes, sir.'

'Well, get Maintenance on to it straight away this time!'

'Certainly, sir.' The guard was almost grovelling.

'Otherwise, before we know it, this place will be overrun by the likes of these two.' The man looked at Sky and Chip as if he had discovered a nasty taste in his mouth.

'We'll see that doesn't happen, sir,' the guard assured him.

'Just make sure you do!' The man stalked off up the jetty.

The guard snarled, 'See the trouble you got us into? Come on, out of the boat.'

They were marched up to a brick building but, the moment they were inside, the big guard lost all interest and said to his colleague, 'You look after these two, Weaver, while I ring Maintenance.'

As soon as he'd left the office, the younger man's attitude changed completely. 'I'll get your stuff,' he said quietly. He quickly returned with their clothes and also a large towel. 'You'd better finish drying off.'

By the time they were dressed, he'd also brought them plastic mugs of steaming soup. 'It's out of a machine,' he apologised, 'but at least it'll help warm you up.'

'Thanks, that's very kind of you,' Sky said. 'We really didn't mean to cause any trouble. We only wanted a quick swim to get the dust off.'

'Where are you heading for?' the guard asked, after he'd written their details down on a form.

'We're not having much success, but we've been trying to find an old friend of ours,' Sky explained. 'He used to be in the Child Protection Unit.'

The guard grinned, 'You don't happen to mean a man called Spindor, do you?'

Sky could hardly believe what she'd just heard. 'You know him?'

'I served with him in the Unit. He was the one who started calling me Weaver, because he thought I was always dodging and weaving.'

Chip looked wary. 'You used to be a Catcher?'

Weaver nodded. 'But not for long, the pay wasn't good enough for the sort of the things I was expected to do. I didn't like the work.'

'I don't see much difference between being a Catcher and what you're doing now,' Chip said bluntly.

'Security here is mostly about keeping out the Skulls. To be honest, we're a long way from the city and we don't usually get many throwaways like you.' He frowned slightly. 'But if you don't like Catchers, why are you so interested in finding Spindor?'

Sky briefly explained they had changed their minds about going to work on his farm and then asked, 'Do you know where he lives? Is it far away?'

Weaver laughed. 'As a matter of fact, when I go off duty in a couple of hours' time, on my way home, I can drop you off at the end of his lane. Mind you, I haven't seen him for ages, but I'm sure I'd have heard if he'd moved.'

Sky and Chip looked at each other in amazement. Chip was the first to speak. 'I can't believe we've been wandering round all this time and then practically found Spindor by accident.'

Weaver said apologetically, 'I'm sorry, but I'll have to lock you in until I finish work.'

Two hours later, they were sitting in Weaver's car and driving along a broad, tree-lined avenue, past large, expensive houses. Although it all seemed very pleasant, Sky could not help noticing the guard at the main gate, who was busy examining a visitor's identity card and checking the details over his two-way radio. She turned to Weaver and said, 'I think this is an odd place. I mean, it might look like paradise, but I'd hate to spend my life shut in behind a high fence, surrounded by armed guards.'

Weaver accelerated up the neat Tarmac drive which led out of Happy Valley and on to the main road. 'These days people are really frightened of each other and they think their money can buy them security.'

'They're right,' Sky admitted. 'Nobody looks after us the way you guard them.'

'The only trouble is,' Weaver continued, 'having all those fences and guards to protect them when they're in Happy Valley makes the residents twice as scared when they leave it behind and come out into the real world. It's a long trip to the nearest city and they're all scared stiff they'll get ambushed by Skulls on the way.'

'What about the children going to school?' Sky asked.

'They always travel in an armoured vehicle, in case they get kidnapped and their parents held to ransom.'

'Funny sort of paradise,' Sky murmured.

'There's always devils lurking just outside every paradise,' Weaver commented and, to prove his point, he directed Sky's attention towards a group of vehicles which was heading down the road towards them.

Even from a distance it was easy to see, by the way the irregularly shaped, fast-moving vehicles snaked back and forth across the white line, that these were Skulls.

Sky, who was staring anxiously up the road to see if she recognised any of them, said, 'I hope this isn't Chains and his mob again.'

'Been having trouble?' Weaver asked.

'You could say that!' Sky replied.

Chip leant forward between the two front seats. 'The lead car doesn't look like his.'

The vehicles were less than a hundred metres away and approaching fast, when Sky said with relief, 'No, it must be another pack.'

Weaver, taking a firmer grip on the wheel, warned them, 'Hold on tight! They're going to play chicken.'

The Skulls' vehicles, four cut-down cars, a huge three-wheel motorbike and several other bikes, had fanned out, right across the road, leaving no room for Weaver to pass them.

Although Weaver slowed down, the Skulls kept on coming and it looked as if a head-on collision was inevitable.

Sky screamed, 'Look out!'

But at the very last second, the Skulls' vehicles parted, charging down both sides of Weaver's car.

Sky wound down the window and screamed at the last biker, 'You're all mad!'

The biker, a fat, red-faced man, merely raised a single finger by way of reply.

Checking in his rear-view mirror to make certain that the Skulls had not done a U-turn, ready for another attack, Weaver pulled over and let out a huge sigh of relief. 'That was close!'

'I thought you were brilliant!' Chip said.

But Sky was less enthusiastic. 'Why didn't you give way? You just kept driving straight at them!'

Weaver nodded. 'It's the only way. When they're playing chicken, if you swerve, you'll probably hit one of them and then, even if you escape, the rest will be after you like a pack of wolves. The only thing Skulls have any respect for is their own set of wheels, because without transport they just aren't Skulls any more. There are a few kamikaze pilots about but, unless you're in something worth stopping, like a Merc or BMW, they usually let you off at the last minute. Still,' he said, putting the engine in gear, 'we'd better not hang around, in case they come back looking for easy pickings!'

Once she had recovered, Sky began scanning the horizon for any familiar sights, which would mean they were nearing Spindor's. Unfortunately, one lot of fields looked much like another. 'I don't recognise any of this.'

'Not far now,' Weaver assured her and, only a few kilometres further on, at a crossroads, he brought the car to a halt and pointed down the side road. 'Spindor's place is straight down there and off to your right. It's quite a way and I'd take you, but our place is a bit isolated and my wife gets nervous if she's left alone when it gets near dusk. But remember to tell Spindor I said hello.'

After Weaver had driven off, Sky and Chip crossed over and set off down the side road.

'I still can't believe we've actually found Spindor after all this time,' Sky said.

'Tell me again about his place. What's it really like?' Chip asked.

As Sky told him about the old farmhouse, the verandah which ran across the front and the purple-flowered plant which rambled across its grey stonework, she couldn't help remembering the idyllic day she had spent there with Spindor exploring the big, cool rooms of the old house. Upstairs, there was a huge, old-fashioned bathroom. At one end of the bath, beneath the big brass taps, there was a lovely enamelled picture of a mermaid with long blonde hair and a silvery tail, looking as if she had just swum up through the plug-hole.

'Just think,' Sky said thoughtfully, 'if it wasn't for what happened to Dig, we could have been living there for the whole of the last two years.'

'But think of all the people we would never have met, like Gentle and Wolf Boy,' Chip pointed out.

'Yes,' Sky admitted, 'but what about all the times when you complained about having nothing to eat? If we'd been working with

Spindor, we'd have had three good meals every single day.'

Chip suddenly came to a halt. 'You do think he'll be pleased to see us, don't you? I mean, it would be awful to have spent all this time looking for him, if he tells us to clear off. Or says he hasn't got room for us.'

'Don't be silly,' Sky said. 'I recognise this bit! Look, there's the turning!'

They broke into a run down a narrow track between high, overgrown hedges. They splashed through the shallow ford which crossed the stream but, as they rounded the final bend, they came to a complete stop.

Ahead of them, instead of the lovely old farmhouse Sky remembered, there was a burnt-out ruin.

The grey, stone walls had been reduced to a pile of rubble and sitting on top of the wreckage, almost unscathed by its fall from the upper floor, was the bath. But, although the mermaid was still peering out from behind long strands of her blonde hair, the bath suddenly made Sky think of a beached whale, which had been left stranded on a pile of rocks.

'I don't believe it!' Sky whispered. Spindor had been their last hope. Angrily, she kicked at a piece of wood. With a growing sense of desolation, she wondered, how much worse could her life get?

Chip walked over to the remains of an upright, which reminded him of the tree-stumps in the burnt-out wood. It rose from the rubble like a charred finger, pointing accusingly at the gathering night clouds. 'Look at this.'

On the beam's surface, which was criss-crossed with lines, like black alligator skin, was the tell-tale green territorial mark of the Skulls.

A voice suddenly barked through the gathering gloom, 'Don't move! My gun's pointing straight at you.'

Eight

'Spindor, don't shoot!' Sky called into the shadows. 'It's Sky and Chip. You remember us, don't you?'

Spindor shouted back, 'Move out to where I can get a better look at you.'

Sky and Chip took a couple of steps forward as a figure, in a grubby T-shirt and jeans, cautiously emerged from behind a pile of rubble, clutching a shotgun. 'You've both grown so much, I didn't recognise you. Besides, I never expected to see you round here.'

'Spindor, is that really you?' Sky was shocked. She remembered Spindor as being such a neat, organised kind of man, but now lank hair hung round his tired, lined face. 'What on earth's happened here?'

Lowering his gun, Spindor said, 'The Skulls raided us. Not just once, but they kept on coming back until there was nothing left.'

'Isn't there anyone else here with you?' Chip asked.

Spindor shook his head. 'Not any more. There were eight kids. We were doing quite well. We grew most of our own food and we were renovating the house. Then the Skulls found us. First they wrecked our crops by driving their machines through them and then they started attacking the house.'

'Where are the others now?' Sky asked.

Spindor inclined his head towards the rear of the ruins. 'The Skulls shot two kids and I buried them behind the house. Then, one by one, as things rapidly got worse, with food running out and the Skulls coming back every night, the others ran away. You can hardly blame them.'

'Why did you stay?'

Spindor drew himself up and looked a little more defiant. 'This is my land, I worked hard enough to get it and I'm not going to let a bunch of Skulls drive me off.'

Chip looked about him. 'Where do you live?'

'In the old barn. 'Come on, I'll show you.'

He led the way, round the end of the ruined house, to a brick-built barn. Blue and yellow plastic sacks hung across its broken windows and the bonnet of Spindor's pick-up truck could be seen through the open double doors. 'I have to keep the truck in there because it's the only building left standing. I managed to salvage a few bits and pieces from the house to make it a bit more comfortable. Come on in.'

Inside, the earth floor smelled of damp and engine oil. Spindor lit a hurricane lamp and hung it from a rusty nail driven into a cobwebbed beam. Leading them down the side of his muddy, rusting truck, which occupied most of the barn, they came to a space at the back. His mattress and some grubby blankets lay in a heap on a groundsheet. Apart from a bench full of tools, there was a rickety table and four broken chairs or stools. On top of a cupboard with only one door, a camping stove was heating a pan of watery-looking soup.

Seeing Sky's critical look, Spindor confessed, 'I don't really like leaving the place empty while I go shopping and besides, I've almost run out of money. So, there isn't much to eat, but you're welcome to share anything I've got.'

'Thanks very much,' Sky said, trying to hide her disappointment. The whole point of trying to find Spindor had been the hope that he would be able to make everything better for them. But even when they were living in a hut on the Tip, conditions had hardly been worse than the ones Spindor was enduring.

'Aren't there any rabbits around here?' Chip asked.

'Sure, but if I waste cartridges shooting them, I might not have enough left to protect myself from the Skulls.'

Sky looked puzzled. 'They've already destroyed everything apart from this place, surely they don't still bother coming back?'

Spindor said grimly, 'Oh, yes, they do, most nights. They say they won't quit until they've got me.'

Sky nodded. 'They said the same to us.'

'I sit up all night, keeping watch, otherwise they'd have finished me off ages ago,' Spindor sighed.

Sky could not help thinking that, in a peculiar kind of way, Spindor was as much a prisoner as the people who lived in Happy Valley, though not in as much comfort. 'Well, if we're going to share your food,' she said brightly, 'at least we can take our turn as lookouts.'

'And we've learnt a bit about living off the land, so we can help with getting hold of more food,' Chip added. 'There's no need to shoot the rabbits, Wolf Boy taught me how to snare them.'

Spindor's face broke into a tired smile. 'I often wondered what happened to you two and how you were getting on. When things started to go wrong here, I was glad, for your sakes, that you'd decided not to come. But it's good to see you again. Tell me what's been happening to you.'

'We'll tell you everything, but to be honest we're both starving. Can we eat first?' Sky suggested.

Later, Sky told Spindor their story. She finished by saying, 'Of course, we've spent most of our time looking for Dig.'

Spindor looked uncomfortable. 'I thought you might. Any luck?' He tried to sound casual, but knew that his part in allowing Dig to be sold to a farmer still left an enormous rift between them.

'None,' Chip replied.

'We'd hardly be coming here for help if we'd found Dig, would we?' Sky interjected.

'I suppose not,' Spindor agreed.

'We only came because we couldn't face another winter without anywhere to live. It's a pity the Skulls got here first!' she added bitterly.

Chip had barely finished an account of their own meetings and escapes from the clutches of the Skulls, when they heard the distant, all-too-familiar drone of engines.

'Here they come again!' Spindor muttered grimly. Grabbing his gun, he swiftly doused the light and crouched beside the window.

Within seconds, headlight beams swept across the transparent plastic sacks covering the windows, as the vehicles circled the yard.

Above the growl of the engines, Chains' husky voice roared, 'There's no point in hiding. We'll get you sooner or later anyway, so you might as well come on out now and get it over with.'

Spindor cautiously lifted a corner of the plastic sack and peered out. While the other Skulls continued to drive round in slow circles, Chains was standing on the pile of rubble which had once been a corner of the house. Slowly, Spindor raised his shotgun, poked the barrel out through the gap and took aim.

'Is there a back way out of here?' Chip whispered.

Without taking his eye from the gun's sights, Spindor pointed beyond the pick-up. 'Over in the far corner, but they won't come any nearer while I've still got ammunition left. There's no need to run for it, you'll be far safer if you stay in here.'

Chip replied witheringly, 'I wasn't thinking of running! I've got a much better idea. When they realise you're not alone any more, they might clear off. Just give us a few seconds to get in position.'

'How will I know when you're there?'

Chip grinned. 'Oh, you'll know! But only shoot if you really have to, because I want us to get right round behind them.'

'You be careful out there,' Spindor warned.

'We will! Come on, Sky!'

Keeping low, to avoid being caught in the searching headlights, Sky and Chip left the barn by the side door and crept round to the far side of the ruined house. When they were directly behind Chains, Chip handed Sky a stone and kept one for himself. 'When I give the word, chuck that at him as hard as you can. Then we split up, but keep on throwing stuff. OK? Ready?' Sky nodded. 'OK, NOW!'

Chip's stone fell slightly short. But hearing the noise, Chains turned round and Sky's stone caught him in the middle of the forehead.

'What the . . . ?' yelled Chains, clutching his bleeding head.

'Run for it!' Chip hissed.

As they split up and ran in opposite directions, they heard Spindor yell out from the barn, 'You got it wrong this time, I'm not alone.'

'We'll still get you!' the Skull roared back.

Constantly changing their positions, Sky and Chip safely managed to keep up a hail of missiles. A windscreen and several headlights were shattered. Several more Skulls, including Pinkie, were injured and it wasn't long before they all decided to withdraw.

Just before they roared off into the darkness, Chains shouted, 'Don't think we won't be back!'

Spindor was re-lighting the lamp as Sky and Chip returned. 'Thanks for your help.'

Chip grinned. 'At least it was cheaper than cartridges.'

For the first time since they'd arrived, Spindor's face relaxed into a genuine smile. 'I quite liked the idea of them becoming targets for stones from the building they ruined.'

But Sky looked concerned. 'How much longer do you think you're going to be able to hold out against them?'

'As long as it takes,' Spindor firmly replied.

Sky shrugged. 'But I don't see what you hope to gain by all this. The kids are all gone, the house is a mass of rubble and you're running out of money. Isn't it time to face up to the fact that the whole thing is over?'

'Never!' Spindor retorted.

He sounded determined, yet Sky could not help wondering if it was only Spindor's pride which prevented him from admitting defeat. Whatever Spindor said, there was certainly an air of doubt and weariness about his every move, quite unlike the way he used to be.

He had certainly suffered during the last couple of years. His dreams had been shattered. Sky could not help feeling sympathy for him, inspite of what he had done to Dig.

Over the next few days, while Spindor stayed on constant guard, Sky and Chip went in search of food. The Skulls returned regularly but, even when they were not there, they dictated every move.

About midday on the fifth day, Spindor was chopping wood for a campfire they had built in the yard to cook their meal, Sky was washing vegetables and Chip was plucking a pheasant he'd caught, when they all heard voices.

'It must be the Skulls,' Spindor said grimly.

Chip said, 'But I can't hear any engines.'

Sky looked doubtful. 'And they don't usually come during the day.'

'Maybe they're hoping to take us by surprise,' Chip suggested.

Dropping what they were doing, all three retreated to the safety of the barn and prepared to defend themselves. But the closer the voices got, the less they sounded anything like Skulls.

'I'm sure I can hear singing,' Sky whispered.

'Me too,' Chip agreed.

'I'm still not taking any chances,' Spindor said, peering through the window, round the edge of a plastic sack. 'They could be trying to trick us into dropping our guard.'

Moments later, a large group of young people appeared.

'There you are,' Sky said with a grin, 'they aren't Skulls.'

'They could be decoys,' Spindor said and, when they left the barn, he made sure he took his gun.

There were about twelve young peopleof all ages. Half of them were struggling to push along an old car trailer and one boy was wheeling a bike, which had been painted in every colour of the rainbow.

Despite their harmless appearance, Spindor spoke aggressively, 'I hope you realise this is private land and you're trespassing.'

A tall, thin boy, whose tight, curly hair was so blond as to be almost white, replied, 'I'm sorry. To be honest, I think we took a wrong turning back there.'

The boy was about to send everyone back, when a girl of about Sky's age, who had close-cropped, dark hair, a healthy complexion and bright green eyes, stepped past him and spoke to Spindor. 'Look, mister, we've been on the road since daybreak and some of the smaller ones are worn out. It won't do you any harm if we take a break here and grab something to eat before we move on, will it?'

Spindor looked unsure.

The girl gave him a brilliant smile, 'I promise we'll clear up any mess we make.'

'Go on,' Sky urged Spindor, 'let them stay. What harm can they do?'

Reluctantly, Spindor agreed. 'All right. But as soon as you've eaten, you go, right?'

'Sure,' the girl said, 'and thanks.'

'OK, everyone,' the boy said to the others, 'we're going to eat here, but we're moving on in about an hour, so don't go wandering off. Did you hear that, Freckles?'

A little boy with bright red hair, flushed with embarrassment and nodded. 'Yes, Suds.'

'We lost Freckles the other day,' Suds explained to Sky. 'Searched everywhere and then found he'd gone down to a stream for a paddle.'

'Where are you heading for?' Chip asked. He'd been examining their heavily laden trailer. Although it was much larger, it reminded him of the handcart they had made for Dig. After Dig had disappeared, they had found it wrecked, on a piece of waste ground.

'Only as far as the next village,' Suds replied.

'While we've been on the road,' Sky said, 'we've never been popular in villages. They don't like beggars.'

Suds drew himself up proudly. 'We don't beg.'

'No way!' the girl agreed. 'We earn our living wherever we go.'

Looking at the mixed group, Sky was puzzled. 'How?'

To Sky's surprise, the girl, from a standing start, suddenly executed a perfect back-flip and then dropped to the ground in the splits. Raising her arms above her head, she proudly declared, 'We're travelling entertainers!'

Nine

'Why don't we ask if we can go with them?' Sky suggested.

While the three ate their lunch, they had been watching the group of entertainers. One boy casually juggled with apples. Flipper, the girl who had done the splits, was expertly balancing a tiny girl above her head. Both had outstretched arms and the smaller girl was poised upside down on the larger girl's hands. The boy with the highly decorated bike was riding it round in circles doing a whole range of stunts, many using no hands. Sometimes the bike was up on its back wheel, other times it bunny-hopped along beneath him, and he could even turn it right round in midair.

Two things had immediately struck Sky – the enormous sense of enjoyment they derived from their different skills and, above all, she was impressed by how well they got along together.

Spindor greeted Sky's suggestion grudgingly. 'You can go with them, if you like, but I've got to stay here.'

Glancing round the pile of rubble, where the house had once

stood and at the land, overgrown with weeds, Sky said, 'Oh, come on! There's nothing left here for you. The house is gone, you've already said you're running out of money and you daren't even go hunting for food in case the Skulls turn up while you're away. You can't carry on living like this for ever.'

'It's something I have to do!' Spindor scowled. 'I won't let myself be beaten by a bunch of Skulls.'

'Let's face it, Spindor,' Sky said, 'they've already won! But at least, if we went with these people, you might be able to earn a bit of money and then maybe you could come back and make something of the place again.'

Chip nodded in agreement. 'Sky's right.'

Sky leant forward intently. 'Spindor, you once told me that if we stayed on the Tip we'd be there for life, and that there comes a time when you have to know when to move on.'

'Maybe they wouldn't want us,' Spindor pointed out. 'After all, what talents have we got to offer?'

Without hesitation, Sky said, 'Years ago, Dad taught me how to do some conjuring tricks. I haven't tried them for ages but maybe, with a bit of practice, I could again. At least talk to them.'

'You can if you like,' Spindor said hesitantly, 'but whatever you decide, I still think I'm going to stay here.'

Sky, ahead of the other two, ran across to Suds. Slightly apart from the main group, he was doing stretching exercises. Pointing at the surrounding debris, she said, 'Suds, as you can see, things haven't gone too well here. We've been having trouble with the Skulls.

They've wrecked Spindor's farm and they they've told us they won't leave us alone until we're all dead. We were wondering if we could join you.'

To Sky's astonishment, Suds suddenly bent over backwards, his hands gripped his ankles and then his head appeared, upside down, between his legs. 'I'm not sure we want to be chased around by a bunch of Skulls. Besides, there are already too many of us. Sometimes we earn barely enough to feed us all.'

'But we could help,' Sky insisted.

Suds took his hands off his ankles and threaded his long, thin arms through his legs and round the back of his head. 'How? I mean, what can you do?'

Hoping that he wouldn't ask for an instant demonstration before she'd had time to practise, Sky replied, 'I do conjuring tricks.'

'OK,' Suds said, 'but just suppose we let you two come, what about him?' Carefully taking one foot off the ground, he pointed it at Spindor. 'None of us are very keen on grown-ups. At best they've never done us any favours, and they've harmed some of us in one way or another.'

Chip spoke up. 'Surely, you get into trouble with Skulls too?'

'Sometimes, when we're on the road,' Suds admitted. 'What's your point?'

'Spindor's got a gun. That would help drive them away.'

Suds looked unimpressed. 'Guns mostly seem to make things worse. Anyway, it isn't up to me to decide.'

Sky was surprised. 'I thought you were the boss.'

'Not really. I make most of the day-to-day decisions, but that's only because the others want me to, because I'm the oldest. When it comes to anything important, everyone has an equal say.'

'Can we ask them about us now?' Sky insisted.

'Sure!' Suds said and, easing his weight forwards, he rolled like a ball towards the main group. He unfolded himself and asked everyone to gather round. He told them what Sky had suggested.

Flipper was the first to speak. 'We can't keep taking in more people. We're already having trouble getting by on what we're able to earn.'

Freckles, squatting on the crossbar of his bike, agreed with her. 'That's right!'

'But, I suppose, if we had some new acts,' Suds said, 'it would mean we could go back earlier to places.'

Flipper shook her head. 'We've never done well by going back anywhere in under a year.' Her tiny gymnastic partner nodded in agreement.

The boy who'd been juggling apples spoke up for the first time. 'I think our biggest problem is the distance between villages. Because the little ones can't walk quickly enough, we're sometimes travelling for two days between jobs.'

'Yes,' said Flipper, 'that's really why we don't get enough money for food. It isn't the days we're doing shows, it's the time wasted in between, travelling.'

'We might be able to help with that,' Chip suggested.

Suds turned to him. 'How?'

'Spindor's got a pick-up truck,' Chip replied. 'Some of the little ones could ride in the back but not only that, you could hitch your trailer to it.'

Before Spindor could point out that he had not yet agreed to go, Sky quickly said, 'That way you could travel so quickly, you might be able to do two shows in different villages on the same day.'

This suggestion drew a buzz of interest until Freckles piped up, 'But then, most of the extra money we earned would go on petrol, rather than food.'

'My truck runs on diesel, which is cheaper,' Spindor said quietly.

Suds slowly started to sound more enthusiastic. 'And another advantage of having transport would be for advance publicity. The kids do hand-drawn posters and while we're doing one show, you could go on ahead and put some up in the next place, so the people would know we were coming.'

'That's true,' Flipper admitted. 'After shows, people often come up and say how much they wished they'd known we were coming, because they had lots of friends and relatives who would have enjoyed seeing us, only they didn't know it was going to happen.'

'That's all very well,' Freckles said, 'but there's still the problem of having a grown-up amongst us. I left home because of what my dad and my grown-up brothers did to me. We've always said we wouldn't let adults in.'

'Even decent adults can be very bossy,' Flipper agreed.

Spindor said firmly, 'I promise, I won't interfere with the way you want to run things.'

But Freckles still looked uneasy. 'You might say that now, but how do we know we can trust you?'

'In that case, why don't we try it? Let them come along for a while and see how it goes?' Suds proposed.

'You mean, make them temporary members of the group?' Flipper asked.

'Exactly,' Suds said. 'That way, they'd have time to learn all the songs and dances . . .'

Chip was horrified. 'What songs and dances?'

'We don't just do our own acts,' Flipper explained. 'Everyone takes part in the rest of the show too.'

'That's what makes our performances better than any other travelling players,' Freckles said. Then, looking hard at Chip, he asked, 'I suppose you *can* sing, can't you?'

Before her brother had a chance to reply, Sky quickly said, 'We both can, like birds!'

'I won't have to sing, will I?' Spindor asked.

With a shake of his head, Suds said, 'We only use kids in the shows and anyway, you'll be away doing the publicity while the show's on.'

Spindor looked relieved. 'That's good, because I've got a singing voice like a rusty gate.'

'Is that it then?' Sky asked. 'Is it all decided?'

'Not so fast,' Suds said. 'We haven't put it to the vote.' Making certain he included everyone, especially those who had not spoken, Suds asked, 'Would all those in favour of these three coming with us put their hands up now.'

Sky watched anxiously as most of the hands were slowly raised.

'Those against?' Suds asked.

Only three hands went up, one belonging to a thickset boy they called Rebel.

'OK,' Suds announced, 'that means you can come with us.'

'Thanks,' Sky said.

'But, remember,' Suds cautioned, 'it is only for a trial period, to see how we all get on together. If it doesn't work, you can be voted out again.'

'How long is this trial period supposed to last?' Rebel asked.

Suds was getting tired of all this talk. 'I don't know, Rebel. I suppose until we decide if they fit in. Now, let's get on. If we're going to eat tonight, we've still got to put on a show before the light goes. Will you three be ready to move out in half an hour?'

'I'm ready now,' Chip said.

'I'll go and put my stuff in the pick-up,' Spindor said and he ambled off towards the barn.

As some of the others began to move away, Chip quietly asked Suds, 'We won't have to sing tonight, will we?'

Suds laughed. 'Don't look so worried! For the first couple of days I think you should just watch the shows, learn the routines and polish up your own acts. Besides, you haven't got any costumes yet, have you?'

he whispered to his sister, 'What on earth made you tell Suds I can sing like a bird?'

'But it's perfectly true,' Sky insisted, with only the hint of a smile. 'When you sing, you sound exactly like a crow!'

Sky looked worried. 'Costumes?'

Overhearing her remark, Rebel interrupted. 'You surely don't think we do shows dressed like this, do you? You'll need to make a proper costume. I think you'd look good in a short skirt. The men always enjoy looking at the girls' legs.'

Flipper slipped an arm round Sky's shoulders. 'Leave it out, Rebel! Don't take any notice of him, he's harmless enough really. I've got a spare pair of tights you could wear with some sort of a top, until you can get yourselves sorted out.'

Half an hour later, when the trailer was hitched up to the truck and Suds was lifting the little ones into the back, Sky saw Spindor looking glumly at the wreckage of his dream project.

'Don't worry, Spindor,' she said, 'this needn't be the end of it all.'

'Oh, no?' he asked bleakly.

'Of course not,' Sky firmly replied. 'At least the land is still yours and if you save up enough money you can try again.'

'And find a way of keeping the Skulls off my back,' Spindor added.

Suds cut short their discussion. 'Can we get moving? Even using the truck, we've got a long way to go to the next village.'

Sky and Chip climbed into the cab as Spindor started the engine. Slowly at first, the heavily laden truck and trailer began to nose its way across the even ground. It splashed gently through the ford and only began to pick up speed after they reached the top of the lane, turning out on to the main road. As it did, the children sitting in the back, the wind blowing through their hair, began to sing in chorus.

Hearing them reminded Chip of their earlier conversation and

Ten

'I think we ought to park right here, on the green,' Spindor said, as he pulled up in front of a row of honey-coloured stone cottages with manicured hedges and pointed at the brightly coloured posters on the telegraph poles. 'This is where I put the placards.'

Suds, resisting the temptation to tell Spindor to shut up, shook his head. 'I remember, from when we last came here, there's some rough ground just behind these houses and we'd be much better off doing the show there.'

'But the green's in the middle of the village,' Spindor pointed out, 'where everyone will see us.'

'That's part of the problem,' said Suds. 'Anyone can see, only the rich live round the green and sometimes people like that don't like us turning up right outside their houses.'

'We'll make more money if we're on the green.'

'Not if they complain to the police and they move us on before we even do the show.'

Angrily gripping the wheel, Spindor hissed, 'We won't earn anything if we're tucked away down a sidestreet and nobody knows we're here.'

Suds remained calm. 'We'll do a full costume parade round the village, to make sure they *do* know about us. That way, we won't annoy the posh people too much and our real customers will know we've come back.'

Sky sighed. During the two weeks they had been travelling with the troupe, there had been an increasing number of tense discussions between Suds and Spindor. She wondered if she had been wise to suggest they all three came along. But she also knew that, in the end, it was Spindor's truck which had got them accepted by the group.

At first Suds had been rather relieved to have some of the pressure of the day-to-day running of the troupe taken off his shoulders. But, as Spindor began to query more and more of the group's decisions, there had been several angry exchanges.

Rebel, carrying the red can which held the fuel for his fire-eating act, strolled up alongside the open cab window. 'What's the hold up?'

Suds said, 'We're just deciding where to set up.'

'Last time we came here, we parked on some waste ground. So, why don't we do the same again?' Rebel asked.

'I was just suggesting we might make more money if we were right on the village green,' Spindor said.

'Last time we tried that in a posh place like this, they made us pay for scuffing up the turf and we ended up with next to nothing.' Rebel turned to Suds. 'Look, who's running this outfit now, him or you?'

Uneasily, with a sideways glance at Spindor, Suds said, 'Me, of course.'

'Good,' said Rebel, 'then let's get on with it.'

As Rebel stalked off, Spindor sighed, 'Have it your way.' He heaved the wheel round and eased the pick-up down the narrow street to a patch of rough ground which lay between a weed-infested pond and a row of run-down terraced houses.

'Jolly looking place!' Spindor muttered to himself.

But the wheels of his vehicle had hardly stopped turning, when a small group of children came racing over to greet them.

'Are you going to do your show again?' the eldest demanded.

Suds smiled broadly. 'Yes, we are. So why don't you all go and see how many friends you can find and tell them we'll be starting in an hour?' As they ran off, yelling and shouting, Suds turned to Spindor. 'I don't think there will be many children who don't know we've arrived.'

'Kids don't give us money,' Spindor insisted.

'No,' Suds agreed, 'but they tell each other and then the other kids will nag their parents to bring them. Then we make money.' He climbed down out of the truck. 'OK, everyone! Unload the trailer, set up the changing tent and be ready for a full parade in half an hour. Flipper, would you and Sky take some of the little ones over the ground and make certain there's no dangerous rubbish in the performance area?'

'And this time, be a bit more careful about picking up all the bits of broken glass,' Freckles pleaded. 'I've already had two punctures this week and I'll need a new inner tube if it has to be patched any more.'

The two girls handed out plastic bags to the younger children and got them lined up across the ground. As Sky and Flipper each pulled on a glove, Suds warned them all to be careful. 'Remember, if you do find bits of glass, or any sharp objects, don't pick it up with your bare hands, just stand by it and get Sky or Flipper to collect it.'

As they set out, carefully examining the ground around them, step by step, even sorting through tufts of grass, Sky reflected on her new way of life. Apart from the disagreements between Spindor and Suds, she was enjoying herself. For the first time since they left the Tip, she was part of a group again and it felt good. She was so relieved to be free of the responsibility for making all the decisions and having to constantly watch out for Chip, as well as herself.

But the best part was doing the shows, especially when they had a good audience who rewarded them with gales of laughter and applause. Nobody *had* to pay to watch. At the end, the performers went out amongst the crowd to make a collection, but people only gave what they thought the show was worth, or what they could afford. Which meant they were often watched by homeless people, many of them children. And, having known how it felt to be out there alone, Sky got enormous pleasure from seeing the expressions on their faces while, just for a brief interval, they forgot their troubles.

During a brief stop, Sky had found a moth-eaten pair of red velvet curtains in a rubbish skip. Flipper had helped her to convert the best parts into a long, flowing cloak to wear for her act. Admittedly her conjuring was not going all that well. Try as she might, Sky kept dropping things and giving the game away. But she had quickly learnt all the words and steps for the routines and was performing them better than some of the more experienced girls, including Flipper.

Chip had no trouble learning the routines but, because of his awful singing voice, Sky had warned him only to mouth the words! When he confessed there was nothing he could think of doing for the show, Flipper, realising that though he was quite small for his age, he was also quite wiry, invited him to try out some gymnastic routines with her partner Gem. To everyone's amazement, including his own, Chip showed an astonishing talent for heights and balancing.

Flipper was delighted by the possibility of extending her act into a trio and, although so far they were only performing a few tricks together in the actual show, the three spent every spare moment practising new and more daring routines. The only part Chip hated was having to wear tights and a leotard.

When Rebel led the parade out round the village, Spindor, still looking gloomy, stayed behind in the pick-up. Rebel, who always enjoyed showing off his muscles, had stripped to the waist and was allowing the flames from the torches he used in his act to caress his naked arms and torso.

Beside him, one of the smallest boys was beating out a tune on a cut-off dustbin, which was almost as big as he was. Next came Freckles, on his multicoloured bike, executing wheelies. Sky, resplendent in her cloak, pretended to produce eggs from her ears, nose and mouth, until she finally dropped the egg!

Flipper, Gem and Chip, in spangled tights and leotards, walked quite some distance on their hands and then did a sequence of handstands and cartwheels, which the girls finished off with a pair of backward somersaults.

As they progressed through the village, people slowly came out of their houses to watch and then eventually joined in behind the colourful procession.

Every few metres, the parade halted while Lefty, the juggler, kept six sharp knives flashing through the air and Rebel ate the fire from his torch.

During one of these intervals, above the hubbub of the parade, they heard two blasts from a shotgun.

Sky immediately said, 'That must be Spindor.'

'But what on earth's he shooting at?' Suds demanded.

Rebel asked, 'Should we go back?'

Suds shook his head. 'No, I'll go back. You keep the parade going. If there is trouble, we don't want all these people being frightened off.'

'I'm coming too,' Sky insisted.

'OK,' Suds agreed, adding, 'but Rebel, keep everyone else away for as long as you can.'

As Suds and Sky ran back, Rebel was already leading the parade forward, encouraging the drummer to make as much noise as possible, in the hope that it would drown the sound of any further shots.

As the two entered the sidestreet, leading to the site, they first heard the noise of vehicles and then two more shots.

'Skulls!' Suds swore under his breath and broke into a run.

They reached the open ground to find Spindor, still in the pick-up, trapped by the Skulls, who were roaring round, circling him.

What was worse, the Skulls had found Rebel's fuel tank and a girl with a flat-top haircut was using the contents to fill up empty drinks cans. She had stuffed the openings with strips torn off somebody's shirt, which acted as wicks. Each rider, as they passed her, took a can, lit the wick and then hurled it towards Spindor. As the cans hit the ground, the fuel spilled out and, as it ignited, exploded in a whoosh of flame and black smoke.

The changing tent was already ablaze but, fortunately, the Skulls appeared to be making no attempt to hit the truck or Spindor, merely to scare him. However, there was still a ring of fire inside the Skulls' constantly moving circle and at the centre of it was Spindor, hunched down in his seat, clutching his shotgun and looking scared.

'We've got to help him,' Sky said.

But, as she was about to step forward, Suds pulled her back and down behind a garden wall. 'There's nothing you can do.'

Sky struggled to free herself. 'But we can't just stand here and watch until they set fire to the truck and kill him.'

Suds refused to let her go. 'If you show yourself out there, they'll only set on you instead. I knew you three were going to cause trouble.'

'What do you mean?' Sky asked indignantly.

'I bet these are the Skulls who've been chasing you.'

'I've never seen any of this pack before,' Sky insisted.

Spindor suddenly raised his gun and fired two more shots. The first went above the heads of the Skulls, whose only response was a chorus of catcalls and a further hail of cans. But Spindor's second shot was deliberately aimed lower and punctured a car's front tyre. The car suddenly swerved out of control, collided with a biker, sending him sprawling from his machine, and then careered off into the pond, where it stuck fast.

Seeing their leader's accident, several Skulls roared with laughter but he stood up on the seat and silenced them by yelling, 'Shut up and get me out of here! Now!'

The girl with the flat-top backed her car over to the edge of the pond and one of the Skulls, with a coil of rope over one shoulder, waded out into the slime. As soon as the rope was attached to the car, Flat-Top revved her engine and hauled the stricken vehicle out on to firm ground.

Far from being grateful, the enraged driver pushed Flat-Top out of the driving seat, yelling, 'Move over, I'm driving. Let's get out of here.' Pausing only to shout at Spindor, 'We'll be back for you lot!' they roared off, towing the disabled vehicle which clanked along uncertainly as the burst tyre slowly peeled off the wheel.

The second they were gone, Suds followed by Sky, leapt over the wall. 'Quick, get some buckets from the trailer.'

Dodging through the band of fires, they hastily found buckets and a shocked Spindor helped them fetch water from the pond to douse the flames.

They were putting out the last of the fires as the parade rounded the corner of the terrace. Rebel broke away and ran ahead of them, towards Suds. Surveying the scorched ground, Rebel demanded, 'What happened here?'

'Skulls!' Suds replied bitterly.

Rebel rounded on Spindor. 'This is all your fault. It's you they're chasing.'

Suds intervened. 'Leave it, Rebel! We've got a show to do.'

Glancing despairingly at the charred remains of the changing tent, Rebel snapped, 'But all our clothes were in there and we've lost the lot!'

'We'll talk about that later,' Suds said firmly. 'At least we're in costume, and we've got to entertain the audience you've drummed up and earn some money.'

'If we get the chance!' Rebel murmured, as two police cars cruised down the sidestreet and parked on the edge of green.

'The police haven't come here to protect us,' Suds agreed, 'but now the Skulls have gone, they'll probably leave us alone.'

Spindor suggested, 'Why don't I get all the cans and stuff they left behind cleared up while you start the opening routine?'

'You'd better!' Rebel said angrily and stalked off to join the others.

Sky said quietly, 'I'll help you.'

As they started to gather up the rubbish, Suds got the rest of the troupe into position in front of the audience. But, as Sky listened to the cheerful song, she could not help wondering how much longer they would be allowed to remain a part of the group.

Eleven

In spite of the raid by the Skulls, the show went surprisingly well. The police stayed for most of it but, when they could see there was not going to be any more trouble, they left just before the end, while Freckles was on.

He performed his BMX skilful tricks, hurtling through the air on a succession of ramps, which he had slowly built up out of bits of wood he had picked up during their travels.

As Sky, waiting to go on next, watched Freckles and his bike spin round, high above the crowd, before swooping down to wild applause, she suffered a sinking feeling far worse than she believed Freckles was experiencing. At that moment, because of the argument between Spindor and Rebel about the Skulls, the last thing she wanted to do was entertain people with her own feeble act.

Flipper, who was standing beside her, said, 'You'd better get your stuff together, Sky, you're on next.'

Looking down at her basket of props, Sky sighed, 'I just don't feel like it tonight, not after what happened to Spindor.'

'You've got to. Sometimes I don't want to perform, but knowing that, if I don't, I won't eat, usually gets me going again.'

Sky protested, 'It's all right for you, you've got a proper act.'

'Especially since Chip joined us,' Flipper agreed.

'I keep dropping things and making a fool of myself. I'm sick of everyone laughing at me,' Sky complained.

Flipper suddenly burst out, 'Maybe that's the answer!'

Sky looked at Flipper. 'What do you mean?'

'If you have trouble doing the tricks right, why don't you take advantage of that?'

'How?'

'Do them wrong on purpose and turn the whole thing into a comedy act. After all, if they're going to laugh at you anyway, why not *really* give them something to laugh at?'

Sky was uncertain. 'Do you think I could?'

Flipper nodded eagerly. 'It's worth a try.' There was a burst of applause when Freckles tilted up the back wheel of his bike as part of his final bow to the audience. Flipper urged Sky forward. 'Come on! You're on! Give it a go!'

Sky never had the chance to decide. As she made her entrance, she accidentally stepped on one of the Skulls' beer cans, which had been overlooked during their hasty clear-up. Sky's foot went from under her, the basket of props went flying and the whole audience dissolved into laughter.

In the confusion, while she was gathering up her stuff, Sky stupidly stepped on the can again, with a similar result. The audience thought this hysterical and Sky's mind was made up. The third fall was planned and it brought her a huge round of applause.

Inside, Sky was glowing with pleasure, though she managed to keep a completely straight face as she launched into her act. But this time, when she couldn't produce the toy rabbit from the hat, she didn't so much look embarrassed as totally baffled. She allowed two more tricks to go wrong before, to her apparent amazement, the rabbit suddenly appeared from nowhere during a card trick. She desperately tried to shoo it away, but it kept popping up throughout the rest of her act.

As the audience howled with laughter, Sky realised that the entire troupe, which normally ignored her performances, had lined up to watch and were enjoying every moment.

Sky rounded off her performance by treading on her cloak as she tried to take her bow and then making one final slip on the beer can during her exit. The applause which followed was so prolonged that Rebel was forced to delay the start of his dramatic fire-eating act.

As Sky came off, everyone gathered round her, slapping her on the back and congratulating her on the transformation in her presentation. 'It was really Flipper's idea,' Sky confessed.

'But you were the one who did it!' Flipper grinned, as they walked away together. 'Go on like that and you'll soon be the star of the show.'

'I'm not sure about that,' Sky said, suddenly remembering the argument between Rebel and Spindor. 'In fact, by the end of tonight, all three of us might be asked to leave.'

'Why do you say that?'

Sky told her everything that had happened while the parade had been going round the village. Especially the way in which Rebel had blamed Spindor for the whole thing.

'Rebel's always been a bit of a hothead,' Flipper commented. 'Probably comes from the act he does. Don't worry, he'll have forgotten the whole thing by this evening, especially if we make a lot of money as a result of your new turn. But how did you two first get mixed up with Spindor?'

'We first met him when he caught Chip.'

Flipper looked startled. 'Caught him?'

Sky dismissed Flipper's concern with a laugh. 'Spindor used to be a Catcher.'

'Spindor worked for the Child Protection Unit?'

'Oh, yes,' Sky said, laughing at the seriousness of the expression on Flipper's face, 'but he gave it all up. He saved his wages to buy the farm you saw. His idea was to provide work and homes for unwanted kids like us. It was working too, until the Skulls came along. You saw what they did to the place.'

'Yes,' Flipper said, rather thoughtfully.

Suds interrupted their conversation. 'Come on, you two, we need you for the finale.'

The collection, when they counted it, turned out to be one of their largest ever. While most people helped pack up the trailer, others went to buy large quantities of food from the late-night village off-licence and grocery store. They drove some way out before finding a decent campsite for the night, in a small, disused gravel pit, and then settled down to one of the best meals they had eaten in ages.

Rebel did not forget his earlier disagreement with Spindor and, as soon as the meal was over, while they all sat round the campfire, he brought the subject up.

'If that man,' Rebel said, pointing an accusing finger at Spindor, 'hadn't been with us, the Skulls would never have attacked us today and we'd all be sitting here wearing our everyday clothes.' Rebel himself had nothing but the jeans he had worn for the parade, although he had found a towel to wrap round his shoulders to keep out the cold.

'To be fair,' Suds pointed out, 'we've warned you so many times about leaving your fuel cans lying around, where people can easily find them. You've got to take your share of the blame for what happened.'

'But the Skulls were looking for him, not us!' Rebel insisted.

'How do you know that?' Freckles asked. 'This wasn't the first time we've been attacked.'

'Those weren't the Skulls who are after us,' Chip said. 'We've never seen that pack before.'

'But this guy Spindor's always causing trouble,' Rebel protested to Suds. 'Look at the argument you were having with him about where to do the show.'

Spindor cleared his throat and said, 'Maybe if we'd done it on the green, like I suggested, the Skulls wouldn't have dared launch an attack, not right in the middle of the village.'

'But at least the site I chose had a pond,' Suds said, 'which helped us put out the fires. We'd never have been able to get water as easily out on the green.'

'We still lost all our clothes,' Rebel grumbled. 'It was lucky they didn't set light to the trailer, then all our props and equipment would be gone too.'

'That's true,' Freckles agreed. 'It's taken me ages to get the stuff together to build all my ramps. If that lot had been burnt, my act would have been ruined.'

'We'd be finished anyway,' Lefty said. 'We couldn't go anywhere without that trailer.'

Rebel firmly stated, 'We said these three could come with us for a trial period but, after what happened today, I think the trial's over and Spindor ought to leave before anything worse happens, even if Sky and Chip stay.'

The argument which immediately broke out was suddenly silenced when Sky said, very loudly, 'If Spindor goes, we go too.'

Sky knew that if she'd said that only the previous day, they might have asked Chip to stay, but would not have minded if she left with Spindor. But after tonight she decided it was a gamble worth taking.

Rebel angrily said, 'You might want to stick up for a Catcher, Sky, but speaking personally, I want nothing to do with their kind.'

A frozen silence fell over the whole troupe, until several of the smaller children wriggled further away from Spindor and some of the older ones flashed open looks of hatred at him.

Sky angrily turned on Flipper. 'Did you tell Rebel?'

Flipper shrugged. 'I only mentioned it.'

Finally Suds asked Spindor, 'Is what Rebel called you true?'

Spindor calmly nodded. 'Yes, I was once a member of the Child Protection Unit. But I hated the way they operated and, after doing the five years I'd signed up for, I left. I'm not a Catcher any more.'

Without any warning, Lefty suddenly leapt on Spindor and rained blows down on him, yelling, 'I was tortured by animals like you!'

Beyond raising his arms to protect his face, Spindor hardly bothered to defend himself. He simply waited until Lefty collapsed to the ground, exhausted and sobbing with emotion. 'Lefty, I never did anything like that. In fact, that was exactly the sort of thing that made me leave the Unit. So I know exactly how you must feel.'

'You can't possibly!' Gem, Flipper's partner, blurted out. 'Not unless it's happened to you. When I was about two, Mum let me go out to play on the street. Some Catchers came along and picked me up, right outside our house. I wasn't homeless, but they wouldn't listen to a word I said. Instead they sold me to a baby farm. One of those illegal places where tourists go when they want to arrange a quick adoption. If I hadn't escaped and if these people hadn't found me, I don't know what would have happened to me.' Gem lowered her voice and added, 'I've never seen my mum since. I was so young, I didn't even know where I lived, or what my last name was. So there's no chance of me ever finding her again.'

'Spindor wasn't like the other Catchers,' Sky insisted. 'I know most of them are bullies, crooks and even murderers, but he was different. When Chip got rounded up, Spindor let him go and he actually rescued me from the clutches of a slave-labourer. I'm sure there were plenty of others he helped too, but he's not the sort of man who boasts about what he's done for others. Spindor only started the farm, using all his own money, to give people like us a second chance. It was a once in a lifetime opportunity to get away from their old life in the city, with all its temptations to pick up bad ways, and make a completely fresh start.'

'The only person he couldn't rescue was Dig,' Chip reflected.

'Who's Dig?' Flipper asked.

Sky briefly explained. 'Dig was a Picker on the Tip and he helped Chip and me by showing us the ropes. If it hadn't been for Dig, I don't think we would have survived. He was always there for us when we needed him. So, when Spindor suggested that Chip and I should join him on the farm, we wanted Dig to come too. He'd always said how much he wanted to live in the country and it seemed an ideal chance. But he wasn't convinced. Anyway, Dig finally went to meet Spindor and talk it over and he never came back. We never saw him again after that.'

As Sky lapsed into silence, the image, which had remained etched on her memory ever after, of the actual moment when she last saw Dig, suddenly came back into sharp focus. She had been standing outside their hut and Dig was way off in the distance, right at the very top of the Tip, on his way to meet Spindor.

Whenever she thought of Dig, deep inside, she always

experienced an enormous emptiness, but this time it was heavily tinged with guilt, mainly for the selfishness of her concern. For the first time, Sky realised that, far from being solely concerned for Dig's safety, she had been much more wrapped up in her own sense of loss. A loss which, if she was honest, she had felt even more keenly than that of her parents. When she decided not to go to the farm with Spindor, it was Dig she'd searched for, not her parents.

Sky suddenly knew, if a magic genie had appeared beside the campfire and offered her the chance of having Dig back in exchange for something vital, like the ability to walk, or to see, she would have made that exchange without a second's hesitation. Indeed, ever since Dig had vanished, there had been a black, aching void in her life.

Rebel snarled at Spindor, 'What did you do to Dig?'

'Nothing,' Spindor replied. 'My partner picked him up. It happened on one of my last tours of duty before I left. Shakey sold him on to some farmer or other, and there was absolutely nothing I could do to stop him.'

Pushing to the back of her mind the picture of Dig being driven off by Shakey, Sky stood up for Spindor. 'He's helped us since and he really didn't have to. With the farm ruined, he was having enough trouble looking after himself; he needn't have taken us in, but he did.'

Rebel was still unimpressed. 'I reckon, once a Catcher, always a Catcher. People like them never change. How do we know, next time we're in a city, he won't turn us in to the Unit?'

'I don't want him travelling with us any more,' Lefty said.

'Nor me!' Gem agreed. 'The idea of being this close to a Catcher again makes my flesh creep!'

'I know what you're saying,' Suds acknowledged, 'but you have to admit, having Spindor and the pick-up this last two weeks, has made our lives a good deal easier.'

'In that case, I think we should vote on it,' Rebel proposed.

'Do Chip and I get a vote?' Sky asked.

Suds shook his head. 'I don't see how you can, not if you say you'll leave as well, if we vote Spindor out.' He turned to the others and asked, 'How many of you think Spindor is making himself useful and should stay?'

Sky watched anxiously as about six hands, including Suds', were slowly raised.

'And how many think he ought to go?'

Only four hands went up and Sky heaved an enormous sigh of relief.

Even so, Flipper pointed out that she had not voted either way. 'As far as Spindor is concerned, I think we should keep an eye on him over the next few weeks. To be honest, I was more interested in not losing Chip and Sky than in keeping Spindor.'

But the following morning, it turned out that several people had voted with their feet. The four performers who had voted against Spindor – Rebel, Lefty, Gem and another acrobat – had all left the camp during the night.

Twelve

'Don't go far,' Suds warned Sky. 'We're only stopping in town long enough to shop for food in the supermarket and then we're moving on.'

'OK, I only want to go for a short walk. Where's the harm in that?' Sky demanded innocently. 'There aren't any Skulls around here.'

'No, but there are Catchers,' Suds said, 'and if you aren't coming shopping with the rest of us, I wish you'd stay in the pick-up with Spindor.'

'It doesn't take ten of us to buy food!' Sky laughed.

Still looking worried, Suds said firmly, 'Fifteen minutes, no longer!'

'OK!'

She watched him lead the others across the hot Tarmac towards the supermarket entrance and then, with a quick wave to Spindor, Sky turned and slowly walked off in the opposite direction.

Sky usually went shopping with the others, or waited outside for them, but this was the first real town she had visited for ages. They had been out in the countryside, with nothing more exciting than open land and the odd little village store. After that, coming into a large town felt like being let loose in a gigantic sweet shop and she could not resist the temptation to explore.

Even in daylight, the vivid neon shop signs seemed dazzling. Everywhere she looked there were huge colourful posters, streets full of bustling traffic and crowds of people. The sheer noise and energy of it all excited her.

But there was also another reason for wanting to get away from the others for a while. Things had not been going so well since Rebel and his friends had left. Nobody had actually complained, but it was obvious their show had lost some of its zip and the collections at the end had got smaller. Chip was getting on well with Flipper, and Sky's own act, now that she was doing it dressed as a clown, was very popular, but nobody could replace the dangerous excitement of Rebel's fire-eating and Lefty juggling with knives.

When Sky raised the subject, Suds had been perfectly reasonable about losing them. 'People have always come and gone. Nobody stays with the group for ever.'

But Sky still felt responsible. She knew only too well that, if she had not introduced Spindor, Rebel and the others would still be travelling with the group.

It had taken weeks of searching through bins, bags and skips, to replace the clothes they had all lost in the fire. Even now, some of them were wearing the strangest outfits. Sky had ended up with a pair of cut-off jeans and a hideous shirt smothered in flowers of every colour of the rainbow. Chip had managed to find a fairly decent old sweater but, much to his disgust, he was forced to wear a pair of bright orange trousers. Even the girls who were near his size refused to swop for a pair of their jeans.

As she wandered down the road, Sky passed shop windows displaying clothing of every conceivable kind. She had grown so used to making do with any old cast-offs, many of which were filthy when she found them, that it seemed astonishing there were still people who actually bought exactly what they wanted. She could barely remember going shopping with her mother.

Sky came to a standstill outside a window with a lovely silky dress, covered in a pattern of rich gold, crimson and brown autumnal leaves. Ignoring the curious stares and mocking smiles of passers-by, she pressed her nose against the glass, drinking in the sheer, impractical beauty of it.

But Sky's daydream was abruptly shattered when an elegantly dressed lady came to the doorway and shouted, 'Clear off!'

Sky briefly held her ground. 'I was only looking, where's the harm in that?'

'You're frightening my customers away and if you don't go, I'll send for the Catchers!'

Scowling, Sky hurried on until she found herself in a large shopping precinct. Along three sides there were elegant shops, arranged in two tiers, and at the far end was a large bronze statue of a soldier on a horse. Some noisy people were sitting on the steps below it.

Near the entrance to the precinct was a shallow pool with a

fountain. As it was hot, Sky bent over to scoop water over her face. As she did, she noticed people had thrown in coins and she smiled at the thought of them making their wishes.

Sky was still blinking away drops of water when an angry voice growled, 'You leave those coins alone – they belong to us!'

Sky looked up to see a man, so heavily bearded and with such a huge mop of untidy hair, he might have been peering through a hedge. What little could be seen of his face was red, his eyes were bloodshot and he smelled heavily of stale sweat and alcohol. He wore a dirty, ex-army greatcoat over a holey sweater and a pair of greasy, ill-fitting trousers held up by a length of washing-line. His grey, bare feet were stuffed into an unmatched pair of trainers and he clutched a bottle by the scruff of its neck.

'I was only cooling off,' Sky explained.

'Ah-ha! That's what you say, but I know different! You've been in there after those coins, haven't you? That's our money. We have that, nobody else.'

'I haven't touched the money,' Sky insisted and she was about to walk off, when the man grabbed hold of her arm.

He thrust his face up close and snarled, 'Then turn out your pockets and prove it.'

Recoiling from the searing stench of his breath, Sky protested, 'Don't be stupid. There's nothing to prove because I didn't touch the money.'

During their short exchange, the knot of people from beneath the statue had slowly staggered across to join them.

The first to arrive was a man in his fifties. His lower half was covered by grubby, blue tracksuit bottoms. From the waist up, he was naked, including his completely bald head, apart from a rugby player's black plastic sweatband, which was stretched tightly round his forehead. His eyelids drooped and his speech was slurred when he asked, 'What's up, Scotty?'

'This girl, she's after the coins from the fountain.'

Sky hotly denied the accusation. 'I am not!'

They all began to crowd around her and, in spite of knowing she had done nothing wrong, Sky was starting to get worried. It was only then that she saw a familiar face, one with a fine web of purple scars down one side.

Even though Gentle's hair hung in greasy rat's tails and the long, white dress was ripped and heavily stained, there was no mistaking her. But she was as drunk as the others.

'Gentle!' Sky cried.

Gentle, her head tilted to one side like a puzzled dog, stared blankly at Sky.

'It's me, Sky!'

Scotty asked, 'Do you know her, Gentle?'

Gentle blinked and said, 'I'm not sure.'

'Of course you do! You healed the wound on my leg. I was with my brother, Chip.'

'Chip?' Gentle rolled the word round her mind. Slowly, a bleary hint of recognition spread over her face. 'Oh, yes, now I remember you.'

'She's all right?' Scotty demanded.

Gentle nodded. 'Yes, Sky's all right, I remember her now.'

Scotty released his grip of Sky and began to wander off, back towards the statue steps, with the rest of the group.

'Gentle, what on earth are you doing with these terrible people?'

'They're my friends now,' she declared.

Sky found it hard to hide her disgust. 'But how did you get into this dreadful state?'

'I don't know what you mean, there's nothing wrong with me.' Swaying slightly, Gentle peered hard at Sky's shorts and highly colourful shirt. 'Are you here on your holidays?'

Sky smiled. 'No, of course not. I lost my other clothes in a fire, but where's all your stuff gone?' Sky asked.

Gentle looked confused. 'What stuff?'

'Your herbal remedies and the things you used to hang on your tree of life.'

'Oh, that!' Gentle looked around, as if she might find it all littered at her feet and then said, defensively, 'I got rid of all that. You go further if you travel light.'

'The only place you're going is downhill! Just look at the state of you and the people you're with.'

'What's wrong with them?' Gentle asked innocently.

'They're drunk and so are you! You ought to see a doctor and have some treatment.'

Gentle suddenly looked unhappy. 'I did see a doctor.'

'When?'

Gentle rubbed her forehead with the palm of her grubby hand, as if this might somehow clear her mind. 'I don't think it was very long ago.'

'And what did he say?'

'I asked him if I could go back to the hospital, but he wouldn't let me.'

'You told us the hospital was closed.'

'Did I? Anyway, he said I couldn't go back and that I had to stay out here.'

'But you don't have to live with those people. Drinking alcohol will do you no good at all,' Sky insisted. 'I know, why don't you come with us?'

Gentle suddenly shrunk away, out of reach, crying out. 'No! And you can't make me.'

Sky did not know how Suds and the others would react to Gentle, but she still persisted. 'I don't want to *make* you, but we could look after you.'

'But I'm happy here.'

Scotty called out, 'Gentle, are you OK?'

'Sky wants me to go with her.'

'Do you want to go?' Scotty asked and, when Gentle shook her head, he said to Sky, 'So, leave her alone!'

Behind Sky, out on the road, a car hooted loudly. Spindor, having seen which way she had gone, must have followed her when everyone came back with the shopping. They were waiting for her. 'Are you really sure you won't come with us, Gentle? You'd be much better off if you did.'

Surprisingly, Gentle appeared to consider the suggestion seriously for a few moments, but finally she shook her head. 'I'd only get in the way. I may as well stay here. They'll look after me. I know they don't look like much, but they're my friends and they take care of me.'

Sky reluctantly gave up. 'Well, if you're sure this is what you want.' There was another impatient hoot on the horn. 'I've got to go.'

Gentle simply said, 'Goodbye then.' She turned and walked off, but then she suddenly stopped, and came back. With a brief glimmer of clarity, she said, 'When we last met, you said you were looking for somebody. Have you found them yet?'

'You mean my mum and dad?'

Gentle thought hard. 'Was that it? All I can tell you is, you'll soon be reunited with someone you haven't seen for a very long time.'

'How do you know?'

'I just know, that's all,' Gentle casually replied and walked off.

When Sky reached the pick-up, Chip asked, 'Who was that?'

Climbing into the cab, and after a backward glance at Gentle, who was already sprawled across the statue's steps with her companions, Sky replied, 'Believe it or not, that was Gentle.'

Chip looked amazed. 'I'd never have recognised her.'

'She's hanging out with a bunch of drunks and she's in a terrible state. I tried to persuade her to come with us, but she wouldn't. She did say one odd thing though.'

'Only one?' Chip laughed.

'She said that, soon, we were going to find somebody we'd been looking for. I asked her if she meant Mum and Dad, but she didn't seem to know.'

Chip scoffed, 'I'm not surprised, if she was drunk.'

'Yes, I suppose you're right. It was probably only the drink talking.'

But, as they left the town, Sky found herself thinking about Gentle's prediction. Although she knew it was probably all nonsense, she could not help being quite excited at the prospect of being reunited with her parents.

At the same time, it also brought back all the resentment, anger even, she had felt about the way they had so carelessly abandoned them. That would probably go, she told herself, the moment she saw them.

That afternoon, while they were driving past field after field of brightly coloured flowers, similar to the ones on Sky's shirt, the truck suddenly slewed across the road and Spindor braked heavily.

He climbed out, walked round the pick-up, and then announced, 'We've got a flat tyre. I'm going to have to put the spare on. Everybody off!'

After they had detached the trailer, while Suds helped Spindor to jack up the truck and put the spare wheel on, the others sat on the grass verge.

On the opposite side of the road, surrounded by a high, chain-link fence, was a whole field full of yellow flowers. Through the mesh, Sky could see the heads of about fifty children slowly working their way between the tall rows of plants. From time to time, they disappeared into the foliage, as they bent down to pull out weeds, which they stuffed into the black plastic sacks they carried.

Sky wandered across the road and crossed the broad verge to the fence. She hooked the fingers of both hands into the mesh above her head and gazed out over the yellow shimmering sea of flowers. In the still heat of the sun, and in such numbers, their oily scent was overwhelming, sickly-sweet, and there was a constant loud buzz of bees, as they moved hungrily from flower to flower.

Some of the children, as they worked their way past Sky, glanced up from their weed-pulling. In the row nearest the fence, Sky saw a little girl whose skinny arms and legs poked out of her ragged dress. There were several livid patches, on her face and others on her arms and legs. Hardly more than five years old, she dragged her sack behind her along the ground.

Sky was certain the girl was about to speak, when she glanced over her shoulder and, spotting a thick cloud of dust moving towards her, she hurriedly went back to her work.

The dust was being raised by a jeep, which shot by at high speed, leaving Sky coughing and spluttering. She was about to cross back over the grass verge, when she thought she heard someone in the field calling out her name.

Emerging through the dust cloud, like a ghost, came a tall, skinny boy with an unruly mop of dark hair. He walked right up to the fence, pressed his face against the wire and, when he saw that she obviously did not recognise him, he said, 'It's me – Dig!'

Sky tried to speak, but found the shock of seeing him left her unable to breathe.

Slowly, very slowly, fearing that the slightest movement of her arm might cause eddies of air strong enough to make the mirage vanish, she raised one finger and, through the mesh, gently stroked Dig's cheek. When she was convinced that he was truly real, tears welled up in her eyes and slowly streamed down her face.

Thirteen

'Oh, my poor Dig! What have they done to you?'

Dig gave her a quiet smile, but she could hear wheezing coming from his chest and his voice was slightly hoarse when he apologised, 'Sorry I don't look my best. If I'd known you were coming, I'd have made more of an effort.'

Brushing away her tears, Sky impatiently shook the fence which kept them apart. 'I want to hug you. It's so wonderful to see you again. From the moment we found your broken handcart on a patch of waste ground, we've been searching everywhere for you, but I'd almost given up hope of ever finding you.'

'I've been right here all the time, promise. Ever since Shakey handed me over to the Boss.'

'But you look so ill!'

'This place is no holiday camp,' Dig said grimly. 'Apart from the guards, they only employ child labour and keep us in appalling conditions, just so that people all over the world can fill their homes with cheap, beautiful flowers.'

Sky, unable to face him, said, 'And it's all my fault. Oh Dig, I'm so sorry.'

'Hey, come on!'

'But, if I hadn't suggested you should go and meet Spindor, you'd never have ended up in this terrible place.'

'Sky, you know as well as I do, kids get picked up off the streets all the time. I was lucky to get away with it for as long as I did.' He broke off and looked towards the distant horizon.

Although she followed his gaze and could hear the sound of a powerful engine, Sky saw nothing. The road was empty and there was no sign of the patrol vehicle.

'Get down!' he said urgently. 'Cover your eyes and nose, take a deep breath and hold it for as long as you possibly can.' He squatted down on the ground, covering his head with his arms.

Puzzled, Sky looked up and saw a helicopter coming over the horizon. For a moment, it hovered above the flowers, like a giant wasp. Then, as it swept low over the field, from bars on either side it spewed out a trail of vapour. The dark, swirling shadows of the rotor blades, which sent the flower heads into a frenzied dance, had almost reached her, before she took Dig's advice.

As the noise of the helicopter faded away, leaving liquid dripping from the drenched flowers, the air was filled with a new sound. It was the buzzing of thousands of bees, bloated with honey, their leg sacs stuffed with yellow pollen, as they suddenly toppled helplessly from the flowers and fell to the ground, beating their wings in a frantic,

131

but futile, attempt to escape the poison before it finished destroying their nervous system.

Sky emerged, coughing. The chemical taste had coated her tongue, dried up the inside of her mouth. 'What is that terrible stuff?'

Dig said, 'Pesticide. It's lethal. They spray all the fields regularly and it gets everywhere. After the first few times you never seem able to get rid of it from your eyes and lungs. You must wash it off your hair and skin the first chance you get, otherwise your skin will start to peel off.'

Sky, remembering the raw patches she had seen on the face and arms of the little girl, was outraged. 'You mean, they always spray the fields with that dreadful stuff while the kids are still working?'

Dig's bitter laugh sparked off a coughing fit. 'Sky, you ought to know by now: kids are cheap to replace. Besides, think of the time they'd lose if they took everyone out of the fields each time they wanted to spray.'

Across the road, Spindor had finished changing the wheel. He straightened up, threw the tools into the back of the pick-up and, without bothering to see who Sky was talking to, called out, 'Sky, we're ready.'

Sky yelled back, 'I'll be there in a minute.'

Dig had been so astonished to see Sky, he had hardly glanced at the other people, but taking a good look at the man climbing into the driver's seat, he said, 'Isn't that Spindor?'

'Yes.'

Dig uttered an almost silent ironic laugh. 'So you still went with him, even after what happened to me?'

'No, Dig,' Sky insisted, 'we didn't.'

'But you're with him now.'

Sky blushed. 'Yes, I know, but we only met up again a few weeks ago. Look, it's a long story and there isn't time for all that now. The most important thing at the moment is to get you out of this awful place.'

'Don't think I haven't thought of it,' Dig said.

'But I remember you telling me how you got out of the Care Camp in a dustbin lorry.'

'Care Camps are like kindergarten compared to this place. I've planned all kinds of escapes, but they watch us all the time and at night this fence is electrified.'

Sky asked, 'Why go to all that trouble if replacements are so easy to come by?'

'Because they don't want us getting out and telling everyone what goes on in here. During the whole time I've been stuck in here, only four kids have escaped. They were all hunted down and killed before they made it to the next village.'

Spindor sounded irritated as he shouted, 'Sky! Everyone's waiting!'

Angrily waving for him to be quiet, she said to Dig, 'Don't worry, we'll think of something.'

'Oh, yes?' Dig pointed towards Spindor. 'And will he help too?'

'It's every bit as much my fault as his,' Sky pointed out.

'Maybe, but he was the only one who could have stopped it happening. Look, it's been great to see you again and it's good of you to say you'll try and get me out but, if I were you, I wouldn't waste a second in getting as far away from this place as possible.'

But Sky's mind was made up. 'Having searched the whole country for you, Dig, now that I've found you, I couldn't bear to lose you again.'

Dig looked surprised. 'Even if that means getting caught and ending up in here?'

'At least we'd be together.'

Dig shook his head. 'You're crazy!'

Sky grinned. 'Yes, probably.'

For a few seconds Dig looked deep into Sky's blue eyes and then he glanced nervously over his shoulder. 'Any second now, you could get your chance to stay for good. Once the spray's settled the patrols start up again and, if they see us, then we'll both be in big trouble.'

'But we have to talk,' Sky insisted.

'You really are serious about this, aren't you?'

'Yes!' she said, rattling the fence in her agitation.

'OK, I'll try and slip out of the dormitory after dark. Moving around inside the wire isn't quite so difficult. Can you meet me here?'

Brushing aside any doubts, Sky replied, 'I'll be here.'

'OK, see you!'

With a brief wave, Dig ducked down and disappeared into the rows of plants. Sky was halfway across the road when a dust cloud, signalling the return of the patrol car, came into sight.

When she got back to the pick-up, Spindor snapped, 'Get in the truck, we've wasted enough time as it is.'

But Sky stood by the open cab door. 'I'm sorry, but I'm not coming with you.'

Chip leant forward anxiously. 'Who was that you were talking to?'

'It was Dig.'

Chip, about to jump out of the cab, said crossly, 'Why didn't you call me?'

But Sky pushed him back into his seat. 'It's too late now, Chip, he's gone. But he's going to try to get out and meet me here tonight, after dark.'

'Then I'm stopping here with you,' Chip said firmly.

'Nobody's staying,' Spindor interrupted. 'You can't wait around here on your own.'

Sky glared at Spindor. 'Frightened that Dig might tell me the truth about what happened that night and maybe I'll find out it wasn't all Shakey's fault after all?'

Spindor shook his head. 'I've always told you the truth about that. The only reason I don't want you hanging around here on your own is because you'll make an easy target for Skulls, or any other crazies there are around.'

Suds leant out of the back of the truck. 'What's the hold up? We're late enough as it is and we've got a show to do.'

'Look,' Spindor assured Sky, 'I'll bring you back here, to meet Dig, after the show.'

'Promise?'

'Sky, I promise. Get in!'

'Chip lost his balance twice,' Flipper complained angrily during the late-afternoon performance.

Sky tried to cheer her up. 'I'm sure most people didn't notice.'

'But it's not like Chip, he's usually so good,' Flipper sighed. 'He didn't seem to be concentrating.'

Sky admitted, 'I've got the same problem.'

'What's the matter with you two – still worried about Spindor?'

'No. But did you see the boy I was talking to this afternoon while Spindor was changing the wheel? That was Dig.'

'The boy you've been looking for?'

Sky nodded. 'He's working on that flower farm and you saw the helicopter that flew over?'

Flipper pulled a face. 'See it? I can still taste the stuff they were spraying.'

'Dig says it does terrible things to you. I saw a little girl whose skin was peeling off and Dig's wheezing. They never bother to get the kids out of the fields before they spray them.'

'That's terrible.'

'I promised Dig I'd find some way of getting him out of there,' Sky said.

'Right now, though,' Flipper said, 'you've got to put all that out of your mind. You're on next.'

But although Sky went efficiently through the motions of her act, she was on automatic pilot. Even while waves of laughter lapped around her ears, images of the little girl and Dig kept coming back into her mind.

Sky was relieved when the show was over and she could change out of her floppy shirt and baggy trousers, back into her ordinary clothes and find Spindor. 'Are you ready?'

Although Spindor had unhooked the trailer, he was not eager to leave. 'Are you sure you really want to go?'

'You promised!'

'And I'll keep my word, but it's dangerous to hang around places like that. If you're spotted, they might have you inside the gates before I could do anything to stop them.'

But Sky refused to be put off. 'I've got to find a way of getting Dig out.'

'Those places have armed guards on duty day and night.'

'But Spindor, we put him in there, so we've got to get him out.'

Chip ran across to join them. 'Don't forget, I'm coming too.'

'It would be much safer if you didn't,' Spindor suggested. 'The fewer people who go, the less chance there is of somebody getting caught.'

Chip said firmly, 'I want to see Dig. He was my friend too.'

'OK, you can come,' Sky agreed, 'but you've got to do as you're told.'

'Sky, stop treating me like a little kid!'

'Sorry,' Sky apologised. As they drove through the evening twilight, Sky desperately tried to work out some sort of plan for rescuing Dig. 'I wish I hadn't done the show. I'd have had more time to come up with something . . .' Her face lit up. 'The show! That's it!'

'I don't understand,' Chip murmured.

'Why don't we persuade the farmer to let us put on a special show for the kids he's got working for him? Then we could find a way of smuggling Dig out with us when we leave.'

Spindor was not convinced. 'Even if the farmer would let you in, which I doubt, you'd never get Dig out with us.'

'There is one way you might succeed,' Chip said thoughtfully.

Sky turned eagerly to her brother. 'How?'

'By using your act,' said Chip. 'You're a conjuror, why don't you *make* him disappear?'

'Chip, I'm only a conjuror, not a real magician,' Sky said.

'You're not very bright either, are you?' Chip scoffed. 'We could make a box with a secret compartment. Then, during the show you ask for a volunteer from the audience to come forward. You make sure that it's Dig, and then make him vanish inside the box. When we leave, he goes with us.'

'That's all fine, but if Dig didn't reappear, the guards would rip the box apart to find him.'

Chip laughed, 'Then you replace him with a dummy, dummy!'

'That's brilliant!' Sky gasped.

But Spindor brought them back to reality. 'I still say getting into the farm is your biggest problem.'

'That's your job,' Sky said.

'Mine?' Spindor sounded surprised.

'Of course,' Sky said. 'You're absolutely right, Spindor. Nobody who runs a place like that is likely to take any notice of a bunch of kids. But they would listen to you.'

Spindor grinned. 'You've got it all worked out between you, haven't you?'

'Of course,' Chip smugly replied.

But Sky added anxiously, 'I only hope we can make it work!'

As they drew near to the farm, to avoid attracting the attention of the guards on the unlit country road, Spindor switched off the pick-up's headlights. He cruised quietly past the place where Sky and Dig had arranged to meet and parked some distance down the road.

Sky and Chip crept back up the moonlit road and sat down in the grass to wait for Dig.

After a while, Chip whispered, 'There's no sign of him.'

'Maybe he couldn't get away,' Sky suggested, struggling to hide her own disappointment.

'You're quite certain this is the right place?' Chip asked.

'One bit of fence does look much like another,' Sky admitted, 'but Spindor was sure this was where he changed the wheel.'

Moments later, they were forced to flatten themselves in the damp grass while the headlights of a car swept by. Fortunately it was not a busy road.

'I'm cold,' Chip complained, wriggling around, 'and I can hear some sort of animal snuffling around in the grass.'

'You'll soon warm up if you touch that fence,' Sky warned.

'Do you really think it's electrified?'

Chip had hardly asked the question when the hedgehog he had heard stumbled into the fence. There were some sparks, a violent blue flash and the smell of burnt flesh.

Sky quietly said, 'Does that answer your question?'

Easing away from the fence, Chip murmured, 'I wish Dig would come. Spindor's going to get fed up with waiting soon.'

'I'm already here,' Dig said, quietly parting the plants and crawling on his hands and knees across the soil towards them.

'Dig!' Chip cried out. Chip was so startled, he lost his balance and narrowly avoided falling on to the deadly fence. When Chip got a good look at Dig's face, looking even more gaunt in the moonlight, he whispered, 'Dig, you look awful.'

'Thanks, Chip. It's great to see you again too!'

'Listen, Dig,' Sky interrupted, 'we think we've worked out a way of getting you out of here.'

Dig patiently listened to their plan but, when they finished, his only comment was, 'Now I know you're both mad!'

'Have you got any better ideas?' Chip asked.

'No. Look, don't think I don't appreciate what you're trying to do for me – I just don't want you, or your friends, to end up stuck in here too.'

Ignoring his objection, Sky said, 'Spindor thinks the hardest part will be persuading the owner to let us in to do the show.'

Dig laughed, 'Oh, no, that'll be easy. The Boss is an old friend of Shakey's and you'll be through the gates the moment Spindor says he used to work with him. Getting in isn't going to be your problem.

Leaving again could be, particularly if Spindor happens to be short of cash. I'm sure the Boss wouldn't mind getting his hands on some more cheap labour.'

On their way back to the pick-up, Sky and Chip agreed not to say anything to anyone about Dig's fear that Spindor might double-cross them. Although, now Dig had pointed out the possibility, they were both worried.

While they drove back to the camp, Spindor raised another problem. 'All you have to do now is persuade the whole group to do a free show in a prison.'

Fourteen

An anxious, hectic few days followed. First, Sky had to persuade everyone else to help. Naturally, most people were not keen to put themselves in that amount of danger.

Having heard the outline of Sky's plan, Freckles said, 'I've spent most of my life trying to keep out of places like that. If you're going to try something mad, I'd rather be as far away from here as possible.'

Flipper agreed. 'I don't even like the thought of being close to it, let alone going inside.'

'Exactly, but Dig's been stuck in there for two whole years,' Sky pointed out, 'and he's very ill. When we first ended up on the streets, Dig helped us. In fact he rescued us. He didn't have to, he had a hard enough job trying to keep himself alive on the Tip, but he did. He never asked for thanks, but we owe him and it's time to pay up.'

Freckles insisted, 'That's your debt, not ours. What you're asking puts us all at risk.'

Suds was also having trouble making up his mind. 'We shouldn't turn our backs on other kids in trouble, but why risk everything for just one person? There are lots of others in there, but we can't rescue them all.'

'I wish we could,' Chip said.

'Some of the ones I saw are much younger than Chip,' Sky said.

'That's fine! But what about our young ones?' Freckles pointed towards them as they sat, silent and wide-eyed, listening to the discussion. 'What if we succeed in rescuing your friend Dig, only to get our own kids trapped in the farmer's net?'

After further heated discussion, Suds was about to take a vote on whether to go ahead and help Sky, when Spindor intervened. 'Whatever you all decide, I've got to help Sky and Chip. I owe Dig at least that much. So, if you go on, you go without me.'

Sky was convinced that most of them wouldn't have minded losing Spindor but they still needed his truck, and it was that which finally persuaded them to vote in favour of helping.

Sky thanked Spindor for that, but he worried her again when he insisted on going alone to see the Boss.

'Why can't we come with you?' Sky asked. She couldn't help remembering Dig's warning about trusting Spindor. She also remembered the phrase Rebel had used: 'Once a Catcher, always a Catcher.'

Spindor's excuse was, 'I want to be certain it's safe before I risk taking you in there.'

Chip continued to protest. 'What's the problem? Dig said all you'll have to do is mention Shakey and then the Boss won't do anything to us.'

But Spindor would not listen. 'Shakey had some decidedly dodgy friends. I used to count my fingers and take a shower after shaking hands with some of them. I've never met the Boss, but I heard a great deal about him from Shakey, none of it good.'

As they watched Spindor drive away, Chip asked, 'You don't really think Spindor is going to set up some kind of private deal with the Boss, do you?'

'No, of course not.' Sky tried to sound confident but, even when Spindor returned with the good news that the Boss had agreed to allow them in to do the show, the doubt haunted her.

Spindor told them, 'The Boss wasn't keen on letting anybody in, but Dig was right. It was only the mention of Shakey which eventually persuaded him. He said we can do it on Saturday.'

'What's today?' Suds asked.

'It's Wednesday,' Spindor replied.

'But that only gives us three days to get everything ready!' gasped Sky.

Spindor nodded. 'I know. What's more, he says the show has to be staged in the main yard, because it's the most secure place, and it has to be put on after dark.'

A shiver ran through Freckles. 'Spooky!'

'Why after dark?' Sky asked suspiciously.

'Because the kids don't stop work until it's dark,' Spindor explained.

'But they won't be able to see us either,' Flipper protested.

'Yes, they will,' Spindor said, the yard's floodlit.'

Having got permission to do the show, Sky still had to work out a way of doing the trick which would allow them to spirit Dig out.

When Sky explained that she wanted to build a wooden box, large enough to provide a secret compartment for Dig, Freckles shook his head. 'It took me ages to find the stuff for my ramps. We'd never be able to find enough wood for something that size in the time.'

'Maybe we could make it out of something else?' Chip said, thinking out loud.

It was Suds who came up with the solution. 'Instead of having to build the whole thing from scratch, why not use our trailer?'

Sky looked puzzled. 'I don't understand.'

'We could probably scrape together enough paint to make it look a bit jazzier, you know, part of the act. And, if we cut a hole through the floor, then you'd only need to find enough old wood to add a false bottom to hold Dig.'

'And if Dig's hidden in the trailer,' Chip pointed out, 'it could be useful if we had to make a quick getaway.'

In between collecting wood and doing shows in several nearby villages, everyone set to work. While the older ones worked on the trailer, the little ones had fun making a dummy. They stuffed some old, sewn-up clothes with dried grass and covered the head with an old T-shirt. Hair, made by unravelling a black sweater, was sewn in and Flipper gave it a face with some of her carefully hoarded make-up.

As the day of the performance drew nearer, Sky began to worry about what Dig would decide to do once he was free. If they would let him, would Dig stay with the group? Or would he want to keep on moving? And, if he chose to wander, would he be willing to take her, and of course Chip, with him?

Having found Dig, Sky was sure beyond any doubt that she wanted to be with him, but from their brief, furtive meetings, she had no way of knowing if he felt the same way.

Sky was tired of people casually passing through her life as if she were a railway station. But then, as a homeless person, had she the right to expect anything more? Was she being stupid even to dream of forming a long-term relationship with anyone? And was it possible that could be with Dig?

Those thoughts were very much in her mind the evening before the show was due to take place, when Spindor took her for a final secret meeting with Dig.

Sky arrived to find him very nervous, so she was forced to stick to practical matters. 'All you have to do,' Sky assured him, 'is to make sure that you get up first when I ask for a volunteer. I don't want to leave the farm with a complete stranger!'

A look of panic suddenly spread over Dig's face. 'But I've never seen the secret hiding-place, how will I know what to do?'

Sky did her best to calm him down. 'Don't worry, Chip will be my assistant for the trick, he knows how it works. Just do as he says.

But, once you're inside, you must keep absolutely still and quiet. It might take some time, because we won't stop until we're well away from the farm. You will wear the same T-shirt and jeans tomorrow, won't you?'

'They might be a bit grubbier, but these are the only clothes I've got, why?'

'Because that's how we've dressed the dummy. Could you wear socks and leave off the trainers? Even if they were willing to part with them, I don't think any of our lot have got a pair like those.'

Dig look worried. 'It all sounds risky.'

'Is it very bright in the yard at night?'

'No, the Boss is too mean to waste money on high-powered bulbs.'

'That's a relief. Look, Dig, I've got to go now, before the guard comes round, but good luck for tomorrow.'

For the first time that evening, Dig's face relaxed into a smile. 'Thanks. Tell everyone I really appreciate what they're doing for me. And that goes double for you.'

'It'll be well worth it if we can get you out of here. Just think, by this time tomorrow, you could be free.'

Dig gave a wistful smile. 'I can hardly remember what that's really like.'

Sky had to ask, 'What do you think you'll do, once you're out?'

'I haven't really thought about that.'

Disappointed, Sky said, 'Oh.'

'I still can't believe it might happen.' He glanced over Sky's shoulder and caught sight of Spindor, waiting in the pick-up. 'The trouble is, whenever I see him, I can't forget what happened with Shakey. I just hope Spindor doesn't let us down this time.'

Dig's words came back to Sky just as Spindor pulled up outside the daunting, tall, double gates of the farm. They slowly opened and an armed guard waved them forward.

Suds echoed everyone's thoughts: 'I feel as if I'm putting my head into a hangman's noose.'

Inside, a vast, fat man, the thumbs of his huge hands hooked into a belt which strained to support his paunch, blocked their way.

Under his breath, Spindor said, 'That's the Boss.'

Forgetting she was wearing her white-faced clown make-up but trying to sound cheerful, Sky poked her head out of the window, smiled and said, 'Hello!'

The Boss merely grunted. His bright red, heavily pock-marked skin looked as if it ought to be sandpapered rather than washed. He had grey, bushy eyebrows and a thin-lipped, cruel-looking mouth, which barely opened when he suddenly barked, 'All you kids, off there and line up where I can see you.'

They obediently scrambled off the truck and stood in a silent line along one wall of the drab yard. Dressed in their bright show clothes, they made a curious sight. The Boss, smelling heavily of cologne, and with huge, damp stains spreading from the straining armpits of his khaki shirt, walked up and down counting. As his podgy finger stabbed towards each person, he mouthed the number.

Sky whispered to Suds, 'I bet his lips move when he reads.'

'If he *can* read,' he hissed back.

When Sky giggled, the Boss strode right up to her and glared at her. 'What's your problem?'

'Nothing,' Sky meekly replied.

'All right, there's eleven of you, counting Spindor. You'd better make sure the same number leave. I don't want any extra mouths to feed!' The Boss threw back his head and roared with laughter at his feeble joke. Two of his guards dutifully joined in with sneering smiles. Then the Boss said, ominously, 'And you sure as hell ain't leaving with any of mine! I paid good money for them, didn't I, Spindor?'

Sky felt a shiver run through her as Spindor quietly smiled and nodded. He was behaving exactly like one of the guards. Was it an act, or had she been stupid to trust him?

'Well, the kids are waiting for you, so we'd better get this over with. Though I can't think why I ever agreed to it in the first place.'

Before she could stop herself, Sky blurted out, 'Probably out of the kindness of your heart.'

The Boss narrowed his eyes at her. 'One more remark like that, missy, and you'll spend the rest of your life chewing with just your gums.'

'Sorry,' Sky said, and truly meant it.

'Get your stuff through into the yard,' the Boss said, nodding his head towards a narrow gap between two tall buildings. Spindor started to ease the pick-up forward, but the Boss blocked its way. 'Leave this here! Off-load your stuff and carry it through.'

Sky shuddered. The thought of having to leave without Dig was too much to bear. She clenched her hands so tightly, her nails dug into her palms.

But Spindor calmly leant out of the cab and said, 'There's too much. It would waste time.'

Without budging, the Boss said, 'The pick-up might go through the gap, but I don't reckon the trailer will.'

Wishing she hadn't been so rude to him earlier, Sky said, 'But I use the trailer in my act.'

The Boss sneered, 'Then you'll have to manage without, missy, won't you?'

'I can't.'

'If it's such a problem,' the Boss said, 'we could always call the whole thing off. I never wanted you here.'

Before Sky could reply, Spindor quickly intervened. 'Why don't I give it a try?'

The Boss shrugged and waddled away. 'You can try if you like, as long as you pay for any damage you do.'

Sky muttered under her breath, 'If the Boss can get through, I'm sure we can manage something as small as a trailer!'

Spindor reproached her, 'If we're going to survive this, the Boss is right about one thing, Sky, you'd better watch your mouth!'

Slowly, he eased the pick-up forward, turning the wheels to line the trailer up with the gap.

'It's never going to go through!' Chip whispered.

'It's got to!' Sky hissed and then held her breath as the vehicle inched forwards. Suddenly there was a slight grinding noise and a flash of red from the brake lights as a front corner of the trailer jammed against the right-hand wall.

'Oh, no!' Sky wailed.

Spindor refused to be put off. 'Look out! I'm backing up again for another try.'

At the third attempt, with only millimetres to spare on either side, Spindor got the trailer through, turned it round under the pale yellow lights of the yard and then lined it up again, ready for Sky's trick and their departure.

Sky could not help thinking, as she helped unload the equipment, that leaving seemed a long, long way off.

While the Boss sat in a huge padded armchair, fifty children were marched in to sit on the bare concrete. They were arranged in rows down one side of the yard.

Sky immediately spotted Dig, in the middle at the front but she was careful not to show any sign of recognition. Sitting right next to him was the little girl with the red patches on her skin. Sky noticed similar marks on several of the other children, including a little boy who had lost all the hair from one side of his head.

As the troupe swiftly set up the props they needed for their acts, there was none of the usual hum of anticipation from the audience. Indeed, if one of them so much as coughed they got an angry glare from the guards who surrounded them.

When one of the youngest artists wandered over to speak to a girl of her own age in the audience, the Boss roared at her, 'Get back where you belong!' and she scuttled away.

The whole audience sat in total silence and, because of the high angle of the pale lights shining down on them, it was impossible to see any expression on their faces. Their eyebrows cast dark shadows over their eyes, turning them into vacant, black sockets.

'This is going to be like trying to raise a laugh in a graveyard,' Freckles complained to Sky, as he began to lay out his ramps.

'I just hope you're wrong about that!' Sky murmured.

Once the show got going, it was not quite as bad as they had feared. After the opening routine, as Suds was twisting himself into impossible shapes, the children soon began to clap, and they loved Freckles' bike stunts.

To leave Dig shut up inside the trailer for the shortest possible time, Sky's act had been moved to the very end of the show, which left her with more time to worry. She was always nervous before she went on, but this time – she was genuinely scared.

In rehearsals, using Chip as Dig's stand-in, the sliding door over the secret compartment had squealed louder than a pig. After they had greased it, the cover, which went over the whole trailer, slipped off, giving the whole game away.

During Flipper and Chip's gymnastic balances, Sky was wiping the nervous sweat off the palm of her hands on to her baggy trousers as she gazed round the yard. The whole thing looked really weird. Even under the dim lights, their stage outfits looked positively gaudy when compared to the drab, ragged clothes of most of the children. Poor Dig was not even wearing a T-shirt.

Sky took in a sharp breath. No T-shirt! Why on earth hadn't she noticed earlier? The dummy, hidden in the trailer's compartment, was wearing one. But Dig was bare-chested and now they would not match! Everyone would know that it was not Dig.

Sky pushed her way through the other acts, who were standing watching. She grabbed Suds' arm and frantically whispered in his ear, 'Dig isn't dressed like the dummy! He's bare-chested!'

'Which is Dig?'

'The big one in the front row. We're going to have to forget the whole idea!'

'No,' Suds said. 'I'll get into the compartment without anyone seeing me and borrow the dummy's jeans.'

'There won't be room in there for both of you and the dummy! Chip had a struggle getting in during rehearsal.'

Suds shook his head. 'I'm a contortionist. I can easily squeeze myself in there. All you have to do is distract their attention while I get in. Then, once Dig's in, throw the dummy away, as a joke. When I come out, I'll go and sit down in the audience on the far side, where the light's bad.'

'But then you'll be stuck in here! Forget it!'

But Suds had made up his mind. 'We can't. You'll probably never have another chance of getting Dig out. We've got to go ahead as planned. I won't get stuck in here, I promise. While we were coming through the gate, I noticed a tiny window in one of the buildings overlooking the road. It's very small but I'll easily get through it, and the best part is, there's a drainpipe beside it and no electric fence.

When you leave, tell Spindor to wait for me down the road.'

'But what about your hair? Dig's is practically black, yours is almost white.'

'Don't worry,' Suds grinned, 'I'll darken mine down with engine oil from the pick-up. Spindor will help.'

Would he, Sky wondered? As she watched Suds disappear round the side of the pick-up, she wished she had called the whole thing off. Now it was too late.

Fifteen

By the time Sky was due to go on, she had been reduced to a quivering mass of nerves.

'I'll never get away with this,' she protested to Chip, the only person she had trusted to keep the secret that Suds was replacing the dummy.

'You've got to give your best performance ever. Remember, it's not just for Dig, we're all depending on you!'

Under her make-up, Sky pulled a face. 'Thanks, I feel much better for being told that!'

'Get on and do it!' Chip hissed.

'It's a good thing I'm wearing baggy pants. At least they might not see how much my knees are knocking.'

In spite of everything, the familiar, first part of her act went quite well. Though Sky could not help noticing Suds, with greasy black hair, was lurking behind the trailer, waiting for her to create a diversion long enough to give him time to crawl unnoticed into the trailer's hidden compartment.

Sky panicked. To distract the audience, instead of going to the far side of the yard and performing a simple trick, Sky went right over the top by attempting to cartwheel across the arena. After three tries, during which she fell over and damaged almost every part of her body, she realised it must have worked. All eyes were on her and there was no sign of Suds.

This is the big moment, she thought, as she limped back to the centre of the arena and stood in front of the trailer. 'For my next and most difficult trick, I need a volunteer from the audience.'

To Sky's horror, a little boy darted out before Dig could get up. Not knowing what to do, she froze.

Chip was the one who rescued the situation. He ran out and catching the little boy, said loudly, 'No, this is a vanishing trick. You're so small, they'll never notice you've gone!' Then, undercover of the laughter, Chip grabbed Dig and dragged him out, saying to Sky, 'I bet you'll never be able to get rid of one as big as this.'

Sky walked several times round Dig, scratching her head and exaggerating his height. While the audience roared with laughter, Dig took the chance to whisper, out of the corner of his mouth, 'Sorry about the T-shirt. Are we calling it off?'

Sky, keeping her back to the audience, replied, 'No, don't worry, it'll be all right. Just stick to the plan.' Turning to face the crowd, she said, 'I might have to make this one vanish a bit at a time!'

She took Dig's hand, which was as damp with nervous perspiration as hers, and led him up to the dropped tailboard of the trailer, which was facing the audience. 'All you have to do is lie in

156

there.' Dig climbed in and lay down on the floorboards. 'A bit to the left. No, a bit to the right.' She seemed to think more about his position, before she said, 'No, lie in the middle.' She picked up a bamboo cane and waved it about beneath the trailer. 'You can see what happens underneath the magic trailer.' She walked round the back. 'And you can see all round it. In fact, you can see everything, so I won't be able to trick you.'

Sky picked up the cover. They had made this by sewing several old curtains together and dying the whole thing black. From a scrap of gold material, Chip had cut a star, which Flipper had sewn on in the centre.

As Sky threw the cloth, with a grand flourish, over Dig and the trailer, she announced, 'And now he vanishes!' The cloth had hardly settled before she whipped it off again and looked surprised. 'He's still there!'

Replacing the cloth, she blamed Chip. 'I told you this one was too big! I'll have another try.'

But when she removed the cloth for the second time, still nothing had happened, Dig started to look anxious. Whilst pretending to share his anxiety, she hissed, 'It's all part of the act. We do it next time.'

Chip stepped forward and suggested, 'Maybe it would work better, if the children helped. Why don't you all shout "vanish", as loud as you can. Let's try it now. One, two, three. VANISH!'

They had added this part hoping that the extra noise would drown possible squeals as the panel slid open.

Chip rehearsed them twice more, until he was satisfied and then turned back to Sky.

With trembling hands, she threw the cloth back over the trailer. This time she shook it, sending ripples running along the surface of the cloth to hide any sign of movement from underneath.

The audience, conducted by Chip, yelled out, 'VANISH!' over and over again, as loud as they could.

They were so loud, especially with echoes coming off the high walls of the buildings, that even Sky, right beside the trailer, could not tell if the panel had moved.

For a terrible moment, she thought it hadn't worked but, when she cautiously lifted the corner nearest to her, there was no sign of Dig and the panel was shut.

Sky whipped off the cover to wild and prolonged applause. She bowed three times and turned to walk off. But, after a few paces, she stopped and put a hand to her ear. 'What's that? You want him brought back again?' She scratched the top of her wig. 'I only said I'd make him vanish, I didn't say I could bring him back again.'

Out of the corner of her eye, Sky saw the Boss was gripping the arms of his chair and looking very suspicious. She quickly said, 'OK, I'll see what I can do.'

Once more she covered the trailer with the cloth. 'Now, call him back.'

They yelled at the tops of their voices and when Sky took away the cover, there was the dummy, looking totally ridiculous without any clothes.

Sky grabbed the dummy and waved it about. 'There's your friend back, safe and sound.'

The crowd laughed, but several shouted, 'That's not him!'

Two of the guards were whispering something to the Boss, who was starting to look angry.

'All right,' Sky said, 'I'll have another go!'

As she covered the trailer for the last time, Sky knew it was make or break time! When Suds appeared, if they weren't taken in by the deception, they would none of them ever get out of this terrible place again.

Her hands were shaking so much they sent waves, instead of ripples, across the cloth. But, before she had time to lift it, there was a sudden bulge and Suds fought his way out. Without a pause, he jumped down from the trailer.

Sky heard Flipper suddenly say, very loudly, 'That's . . .'

Sky quickly cut her off. ' . . . amazing! Yes, I know, thank you!'

As Suds rejoined the crowd, at the darkest end of the yard and furthest from the Boss, Sky couldn't help seeing a thin trickle of black oil, running down the back of his neck and on to his bare back.

Sky shot a quick look at the Boss, but he was laughing and clapping with the rest and she sighed with relief as the troupe moved swiftly into their finale.

Knowing that the sooner they got out the better, everyone was piling their props back into the trailer almost before the last echoes of the applause had died away.

But the happy, carefree atmosphere generated by the

entertainment swiftly disappeared. The children who, only moments earlier, had been laughing and clapping, were soon marched away, heads down, in silent lines.

Suds was next to last in line and Sky felt a little happier when she saw the girl behind him look around to check that none of the guards was watching and then, with one quick movement of her hand, wipe the trail of oil from his back and neck. It was comforting to think that at least none of the children would give Suds away to their captors.

Even so, as the Boss hauled himself up, Sky was terrified that he might have worked out the trick she had played on him.

Sky had almost reached the truck when she suddenly realised that the Boss would not have to work out the trick! With Suds gone, they were going to be one short when he counted them before allowing them to leave.

She raced over to Spindor, gripped his arm and whispered, 'We'll never get out – we're one short with Suds missing.'

Spindor quickly raised a finger to his lips. 'It's all taken care of. Just don't crush your friend when you climb into the cab.'

Sky was astonished to see that Spindor had recovered the dummy, draped his coat round its shoulders and even found a hat, which was pulled well down to hide the painted face.

'We'll never get away with this!'

As Spindor bundled her into the cab and slammed the door, he said, 'We've no other hope.' He turned to the others and barked, 'Come on you lot! It's late and I'm tired. If you aren't on board in ten seconds, I'm leaving without you.'

As they all scrambled into the truck, the Boss ambled across and stood by Spindor's open window. 'Not so fast! I've still got to count you all. We don't want you leaving with any stowaways, do we? Out you get and line up by the wall.'

Sky held her breath. If the Boss insisted, the game was over.

'Have a heart,' Spindor said. 'Can't you see they're all worn out.'

In the silence which followed Sky, with the dummy squashed between Spindor and herself, began to shake with fear. She shook so badly that the dummy's head jerked forward and its hat began to slide down over its face. Sky did not trust herself to try and stop it, even though she knew if it slipped much further it would fall off altogether.

Spindor jammed his shoulder against the dummy. 'Look, this one's nearly asleep already.'

Reluctantly, the Boss relented. 'OK. Whatever!' Slowly he walked round the truck counting them all. While he was walking across the front counting the three sitting in the cab, Sky thought she was going to be sick.

Worse was to come. 'I reckon you're one short,' he announced. 'Eleven of you came in, now there's only ten.'

Spindor leapt out of the cab, leaving Sky to grab the dummy and keep it in place, and said, 'There's three of us in the front, so there must be eight in the back.' Spindor looked in the truck and hauled up Freckles, who had fallen asleep, out of sight, on the floor. 'You missed this one!'

'OK, on your way,' the Boss said and turned his back on them.

Freckles mumbled sleepily, 'Don't bother to thank us or anything.' Fortunately the Boss was out of earshot.

'Come on, let's get moving!' Sky urged, longing to be outside the gate.

But Spindor seemed in no hurry as he calmly climbed back in. He started the engine and whispered, 'No point in rushing things. We've still got to make it through that narrow gap yet. Having got this far, I don't want to rip the side off the trailer and have Dig fall out in the yard!'

Once more Sky held her breath as the vehicle inched forward and she did not relax until they had got through and the gate clanged to behind them.

When they were some distance up the road, everyone let out a massive cheer and they began to sing songs from their show.

Even the normally straight-faced Spindor allowed himself a grin of admiration. 'You carried that off pretty well.'

And Sky, wondering how she could ever have doubted him, grinned back. 'Thanks.'

'I must say, I was really worried when Suds came and asked me for some engine oil for his hair. I never thought you'd get away with that!'

'Nor me! But it's not over yet,' Sky reminded him.

'So, what's the plan now?'

'First, we drive down the road and let Dig out. He must be sweating like a pig, cramped up in there.'

After a few kilometres, Spindor pulled off into a lay-by and they quickly unloaded everything on to the grass verge. But when Sky tried to slide the panel across it jammed.

'Get me out of here!' Dig pleaded.

'We're trying!' Chip promised.

'Thank goodness this didn't happen during the show,' Sky muttered, struggling to free it.

'Everything else did!' said Freckles.

'And what's going to happen to Suds?' Flipper demanded.

The others, who still did not know about the last minute change of plan, crowded round. While Sky tugged at the stuck door, she explained exactly what had happened.

'That's it!' she cried in triumph, as the make-shift door finally moved and a hot, sticky Dig crawled out of the confined space. She threw her arms round him, but then pulled away and asked, 'Why on earth weren't you wearing your T-shirt? You nearly ruined everything'

'I know,' Dig said, shamefaced. 'This afternoon one of the kids had an accident. He caught his hand in the cutting machine we use for making flower boxes.'

'Poor kid!'

'One of the guards just ripped off my T-shirt and used it to stop the blood dripping on the pile of cardboard. I couldn't wear it covered in blood.'

'At least it all worked out in the end,' Sky sighed.

Chip, with a grin so wide, it almost split his face in two, said to Dig, 'It's great to see you out of there.'

'That's all very well,' Flipper interrupted, 'but what about Suds?'

Brought back down to earth, Sky sighed deeply. 'There's nothing we can do for him, except wait and hope.'

After everything was loaded back into the trailer, they waited for over an hour. Spindor was sitting in the cab of the pick-up, with the lights off, while everyone else was lying hidden in the deep grass behind the lay-by. That part was Spindor's idea. 'Just in case they discover Dig's missing and come after us. At least, if you're off the truck, you can split up and make a run for it and I'll be the only one who gets caught.'

Everyone was starting to get anxious. First one and then another would kneel up and peer into the darkness for any sign of Suds.

'He should be here by now,' Freckles whispered.

'They must have caught him.' Flipper was starting to sound resigned to the idea.

Sky insisted, 'We can't give up hope yet.'

She suddenly felt someone reach out to her through the darkness and Dig's hand clasped hers in a firm squeeze of encouragement. She was even more pleased when he did not let go again. It was so comforting to have him back beside her, and silent tears of relief started to trickle down her cheeks, over the remains of her clown make-up.

Dig's breath tickled her ear as he whispered, 'Why are you crying?'

'Only because I'm so glad it's almost over, and that you're here.'

'Me too,' Dig replied.

Another hour passed, before Freckles gasped, 'Listen! What's that?'

Everyone listened. But instead of the sound of just the one pair of feet they had been expecting to come up the road, there were several.

'It must be the guards,' Flipper hissed.

'Keep down until we're certain,' Freckles said.

'If it is the guards,' Flipper reminded them, 'split up and run for it!'

They crouched down, peering through the darkness, straining their eyes to try and make out the approaching figures.

A voice cut through the gloom. 'If this is a surprise party, forget it, I'm bushed.' It was Suds!

As they all leapt out of hiding, Suds introduced them to his companions. 'These are Midge and Supermouse.' It was the little girl with the scarred face and arms, and the half-bald boy. 'After they risked showing me how to find the window, I hadn't the heart to leave them behind.'

Spindor interrupted the greetings. 'I think we've hung around here long enough. Let's get going!'

Once everyone had scrambled aboard, Spindor drove through the night to put as much distance as possible between them and the Boss.

Sixteen

During the days and weeks following Dig's rescue, as the first frosts of autumn scorched the leaves into vivid shades of orange and gold, everything else changed too.

In spite of several minor brushes with the Skulls, the group slowly became far more successful than it had ever been. Not long after rescuing Dig, they came across Rebel and Lefty.

Things had not gone well for them. In the first week away from the others, Gem had been kidnapped. The rumour was that she was sold to a man who uses children to make carpets, because their fingers are nimble and small, and the poor conditions in his factory ruin their eyesight. Rebel and Lefty had tried to perform in the city streets, but when they were not being moved on by the police, or harassed by Catchers, they were robbed of what little money they collected by other street-kids.

When they heard how Spindor had succeeded in proving himself by helping with Dig's escape, the two were impressed, and agreed to rejoin the group.

Their acts strengthened the group's appeal and soon they were not simply able to feed themselves, but they were regularly dividing up surplus cash. After an initial mini spending spree, because this was a new situation, and one which nobody believed would last, most people started to save their money.

Midge quickly teamed up with Flipper and Chip while Supermouse, wearing a fright-wig over his bald patch, made a wonderful little clown, adding to the fun of Sky's act.

But, although it had taken an enormous amount of time and effort to build, Sky could not bring herself to use the secret compartment in the trailer as a regular part of her act.

'After all,' she said, 'you never know when we might need it again.'

To Sky's relief, Dig did decide to stay with the group. In fact, he had little choice. He was far sicker, from the effects of two years of being regularly sprayed with the pesticide, than she had realised. Any strenuous activity caused him to suffer serious breathing difficulties and coughing fits.

Dig helped with as many odd jobs as he could, did more than his share of the cooking and surprised everyone, including Sky, by revealing an unexpected talent for music. With great skill and patience he made himself a set of pipes by hollowing out different lengths of bamboo cane which he bound together with string. He played them during the shows, finding appropriate tunes for some of the acts. For Sky, he produced very jolly music, but it was the slow, haunting melodies he played for Flipper's act which lingered on in the mind long after the last notes had died away.

After one performance, as she listened to the notes soaring into the sky and diving back down to earth, Sky gasped, 'I had no idea you were musical.'

'I'm not,' Dig shrugged, 'I can't read a note.'

'But you remember all those beautiful tunes.'

'No, I don't. I just watch what people are doing and make the tunes up as I go along. I first started playing when my mum was ill. She was in terrible pain and I used to make up tunes to take her mind off it. Sometimes I played for hours on end, until my lips were sore, but I stopped when she died and I haven't played since, not until now.'

Dig wanted to write a newspaper article about his experiences on the flower farm. Sky helped, because Dig had never learnt to read or write, but she was not convinced that anyone would take any notice. 'You're always saying nobody cares what happens to wastelanders or throwaways.'

'I know,' Dig admitted, 'but we've got to start somewhere, and maybe if we got hold of a camera and took pictures of Midge and Supermouse, people might begin to realise what's happening to us out here in the real world.'

Beacause Chip was very busy, rehearsing new and ever more dangerous and spectacular balances with Flipper and Midge, Dig spent all his spare time with Sky. In spite of his weakened condition, having Dig beside her gave her a strength and confidence in herself she had not felt since the terrible moment when she woke up and found her parents had gone.

One morning, the trio was rehearsing and Dig was coughing badly over his notes for his article. Sky suddenly said, 'Gentle would have found something to treat you. She always had wonderful herbal remedies. She could clear up Midge's skin, make Supermouse's hair grow and probably help your breathing too.'

Dig looked up from his notes. 'Who is Gentle?'

Sky told him the whole story, ending with their last meeting. 'It was the same day I found you. I remember now! She predicted I was going to meet you. She said I'd find somebody I was looking for and I thought she meant my parents, but it was you. She was with a bunch of drunks and was in a dreadful state.'

'Why don't we go and find her?'

'And then what?'

Dig gave her a quiet smile. 'Rescue her of course. You've got rather good at that kind of thing.'

'What if she doesn't want to be rescued?'

Dig considered this possibility for a moment and then replied, 'Kidnap her! After all, it's for her own good!'

That afternoon Spindor, Sky, Dig and Chip set out in the pick-up and drove back to the town where they had last seen Gentle.

'This is crazy!' Sky said, as they pulled up alongside the square. 'She's probably been moved on, or arrested, weeks ago.'

'No, she hasn't!' Chip said. He pointed out the group of people, still sitting on the steps below the horse, as if they had never moved from the spot. Gentle sat in the middle, her head propped up against the horse's bronze foreleg. Her scarred face was streaked with dirt and her hair hung in lank strands. The old raincoat she wore gaped open to reveal the tattered remnants of her once white dress.

'OK,' Spindor said. 'Let's do it!'

The four marched across the square and pushed their way through to Gentle.

Looking up at Spindor through an alcoholic haze, to everyone's surprise, Gentle welcomed him like a long-lost friend. 'Hi, where are your sunglasses?'

Sky was amazed. 'Gentle once said she knew you, but I didn't really believe her.'

Spindor nodded. 'Oh, it's true, though I wouldn't have recognised her in this state and I never knew her name. During my early days at the farm, she turned up and stayed for a couple of days. She cooked us some terrific herb omelettes but then, one morning we woke up to find she'd left.'

Spindor bent down and hoisted Gentle up in a fireman's lift. Upside down, she feebly beat at his back, as they passed bewildered shoppers on their way back to the pick-up. Scotty and the others bellowed their protests and Scotty even tried to follow them, but he was too drunk and collapsed in a heap beside the fountain.

'Until she's cleaned up, Gentle will have to go in the back because she stinks!' Spindor said, dumping her like a sack.

'I'd better go with her,' Sky volunteered, 'to make sure she doesn't fall out.'

As they sped out of town, Gentle drunkenly thrashed around, wailing, 'What are you doing? Where are you taking me? I want to get off!'

Sky dodged her flailing arms and refused to let her go.

When they got Gentle back to camp, Sky soon began to wonder if the whole thing had been such a good idea. Gentle yelled and screamed at everyone and it took several of the girls to get her undressed and into a nearby river, where they scrubbed her body and hair. When she was dry, Gentle continually scratched and spat at everyone when they put her in different, ill-fitting clothes.

'These will have to be burned!' Flipper held Gentle's smelly garments at arm's length.

But Sky took the dress from her. 'You can't burn this.'

'It's not fit to wear.'

'I'll wash it.'

Flipper scoffed, 'It's full of holes.'

But Sky refused to be put off and, while Gentle sat around hugging herself and swearing at anyone within earshot, she spent her free time washing it clean and trying to sew up the ragged material.

It took several agonising weeks of fighting, sweating and screaming before the effects of the alcohol left Gentle's system. Not until the craving for drink had disappeared completely did she get any quieter.

Eventually she became totally silent. She would sit for hours on end, staring into space. She did not eat anything and hardly drank any of the water they offered her. When they wanted to move sites, they hauled her up, put her in the pick-up and unloaded her at the new site like one of the props. But, for the most part, she simply sat and stared.

Then as if by magic, one day, as Midge went by, Gentle suddenly said, 'You ought to put something on those scars, to help them heal and take out the poison.'

Anxiously, as Sky watched Gentle wander off, she wondered, 'Do you think she'll ever find her way back?'

But she need not have worried. Gentle returned carrying a large assortment of leaves. She calmly borrowed a pan and brewed up a particularly evil-smelling potion.

'That's more like the old Gentle,' Sky sighed and she handed over the repaired dress, which Gentle changed into without a word.

A kind of selective time-switch seemed to have been triggered in Gentle's brain. She talked again of the hospital she had been in as a child, but appeared to remember nothing of the time she had spent with Scotty and his friends. She seemed truly to believe she had never been apart from Sky and Chip. The only thing that was missing was her tree of life, but Gentle soon began to collect new objects, which decorated the leafless trees of their various campsites.

Her first, foul-smelling potion did begin to soothe Midge's skin and it slowly healed over. Gentle also made up a concoction for Dig to inhale, which eased his breathing problems, but the long-suffering Supermouse obstinately stayed bald, whatever ghastly substances Gentle rubbed in, or smeared across his scalp.

They were passing through a town on their way to a new venue, when Spindor casually asked, 'Sky, have you any idea of where you are?'

'No. I seem to have been going round in circles for ages.'

'This is the city where we first met.'

Sky looked around her, at the shops and buildings, but recognised nothing. 'You mean the Tip I worked on with Chip and Dig is near here?'

'Yes,' Spindor grinned. 'You want me to drop you off?'

For a fleeting second, Sky had a strong urge to go and look round her old haunts and find out who was living in their old hut. Maybe Berry would still be around. But she quickly pushed away the temptation.

'No,' she said. 'Some things are best left alone. I don't want to go back.'

'I wouldn't mind,' Spindor said.

Sky was shocked. 'You want to go back to the Tip? Or to being a Catcher?'

Spindor shook his head, 'Neither of those! No, I want to go back to my farm, or what little's left of it by now.'

Sky understood. She thought that if there had been the slightest possibility of returning to her last real home, with Mum and Dad, she would probably have taken it. 'Are you getting tired of travelling around and seeing new places all the time?'

'A bit. I just have this hankering to get back there and have one more try. You know?' He turned to look at Sky.

'Yes, but look where you're going right now!' Sky said.

Spindor, calmly swerving to avoid an on-coming truck, continued, 'Maybe, now I know what I'm up against, I could make a better job of it.'

'Spindor, look where you're going!'

'Sorry.'

'Have you got enough money to survive back there again?'

'I've saved up quite a lot over the last few weeks and maybe I can find some kind of part-time job which would help out. I'd probably have to make do with living in the barn for a while longer, but I'd fix it up better than it was.'

'But everyone's going to be very upset if you leave,' she pointed out.

'They weren't that keen on me joining!'

'But they've got used to you now,' Sky said, 'and they'll really miss you and the pick-up.'

'Would you and Chip come back with me?'

When Sky did not immediately reply, Spindor turned to see the expression on her face.

'Look out!' Sky shrieked.

Spindor braked just too late to avoid hitting a woman who was crossing the road. But, while everyone else leapt out and went to help the woman, who was still lying in front of the pick-up, Sky stayed in the cab, breathless and shaking.

In the split-second before Spindor hit the woman, Sky had caught a brief glimpse of a pair of intensely brown eyes, which instantly reminded her of Chip's. Sky was convinced that the woman lying on the road was her mother. Any moment she expected Chip to come running back and confirm her belief.

Even though it had taken some time, Gentle's prediction had

meant finding their parents. So, why wasn't she out there with the others?

Sky forced herself to climb down and, still shaking, she joined the rest. As she did, the woman, who had been lying face down, slowly rolled over and Sky found herself looking down at a complete stranger. Sky was terribly shocked by the enormous wave of relief which passed over her.

'My head hurts,' the woman groaned, touching a blue and green lump, the size of a hen's egg, on her forehead.

As a Catcher, Spindor had been trained in first-aid. He checked her over for serious injuries before helping her up and through the knot of people. He had hardly sat her down on the pavement when a Catcher's van, seeing the crowd of children, pulled up behind the pick-up.

Two Catchers forced their way through the group, immediately grabbed hold of a child in either hand and began to drag Midge, Supermouse, Freckles and Flipper, back towards their van's rear doors. The four struggled and protested. One of the Catchers drawled, 'Come on! There's no point in trying to escape. We've got you and you're coming with us.'

Spindor stepped forward, put a hand on the van door to prevent it opening, and said, 'Officer, all these kids are with me.'

The Catcher who had hold of Midge and Supermouse, laughed, 'Oh, sure! And who are you, the Pied Piper?'

The second Catcher did not smile as he tried to use Freckles to push Spindor aside. 'Mister, I don't care who you are. If you don't get your hand off that door and let us do our job, I'll have you arrested too.'

Spindor grabbed the man by the tie and thrust his head back fast, until there was a hollow thud as it hit the van door. 'I'm Spindor! Remember the name, because it could cost you your job.'

The first Catcher, startled by the strength of Spindor's anger, let go of Midge and Supermouse, who darted back to Sky. 'Look,' he said to Spindor, 'I don't know who you are, but we're only doing our jobs. People like you are always complaining about what the street-kids get up to. You say something should be done but, when it comes to it, you just can't stomach seeing it.'

Spindor, who still had the other Catcher pinned up against the van, snarled, 'You are supposed to be Child Protection Officers. Getting the kids off the streets is only part of your job, but it's what happens to them afterwards that concerns me.'

The Catcher, who was having difficulty breathing, spluttered, 'And what would you know about that?'

Spindor, hitting the man's head against the van with each word, said, 'Everything! Tell your colleague, Shakey, you met Spindor!'

Light dawned on the man's face. 'You're Shakey's old partner, aren't you?' He instantly released Freckles and Flipper. 'Hey, look, we didn't know . . .'

Spindor released his grip on the man, but thrust his face up close to him. 'You didn't ask, you just grabbed! I told you these kids were with me, but you wouldn't listen. Picking up homeless kids is one thing, but not when they're under the supervision of a responsible adult.'

'You don't look so responsible to me!' he replied, but when Spindor made another grab for his throat, he dodged away. 'Hey, all right! Only kidding!' Turning to his partner, he said, 'Come on, let's get out of here!'

As the Catcher's van drove away, they discovered that, during all the fuss, the injured woman had gone too.

Spindor drove very carefully out of town. Sky stared straight ahead, struggling to come to terms with the confused thoughts and feelings she had experienced while she believed the woman was her mother.

While they were setting up the flares which would light up the late afternoon show, instead of sharing her thoughts with Chip, she turned to Dig. 'For a second, I thought it was Mum we'd run down. I was so mixed up. Part of me wanted it to be Mum and the rest of me was scared that it would be.'

'You mean, you were frightened that we'd killed her?' Dig asked.

'No, and that's what's so awful. I hardly thought about whether she was dead or alive. My whole mind was taken up with wondering if I wanted to meet her again. But that's stupid! Ever since we split up, I've dreamed about Mum and longed to be back with her. I've always thought, if only I could go back to the old days.'

Dig suggested, 'Maybe that's the problem. Much as you think you might like to, in real life, you can't push back the hands of the clock. Too much has happened to everyone since you separated. You aren't the person your mother left in that car and she wouldn't be the same either. I've known throwaways who've found their parents after years apart. They're ecstatic when they first meet, but it usually doesn't take long before they find out they've become total strangers.'

'That can't be true!' Sky insisted.

'I'm afraid it is. Believe me, Sky, since we first met, you've grown into a completely different person. You've grown up and the time for you to meet your parents again has long since passed.'

As Sky put on her costume, she thought maybe Dig was right. Perhaps, as far as her parents were concerned, it was time to let go and get on with her own life.

Seventeen

Several days later, during breakfast, Spindor suddenly announced to everyone, 'I've decided to go back to the farm. I don't like walking out on you all but it's something I've got to do and if I don't do it soon, I never will.'

After a good deal of protest, Suds said, 'I suppose we always knew you'd leave sooner or later.'

'I'm sorry to leave you without transport.'

'We managed before, remember?' Freckles said.

'And I really hate the idea of not seeing any of you again,' Spindor added.

'It doesn't have to be like that,' Suds replied. 'We always have a hard time getting by in the middle of winter. Maybe when the weather gets really bad and people don't want to stand around in the cold watching us, you'd let us come and stop at your place for a couple of months. We'd try and earn our keep. Perhaps we could find a hall somewhere and do a show during the Christmas holidays.'

Spindor smiled, 'You'd be welcome, all of you, any time.'

Chip asked, 'What about the Skulls?'

Spindor shrugged. 'I'll just have to think of something, but, if I let them drive me off my own land, I'd have trouble looking myself in the eye while I'm shaving. The question is, and I don't want to split up the group, but does anyone else want to come with me?'

Sky knew, when he posed the question, he was looking straight at her, but she avoided his gaze and did not answer. The meeting ended with nothing decided, except that Spindor would definitely be leaving for the farm at the end of the week.

'What are we going to do?' Sky asked Chip.

Chip looked sullen. 'What do you mean by we? You can make your own mind up. Besides, I don't have to do what you want.'

Sky was puzzled, he had never talked this way before. 'No, of course not. But at least we should talk about it.'

'Why? So that you can persuade me?' Chip asked stubbornly.

'Chip, whatever's the matter with you? All the time we've been alone, we've worked everything out together. Why should this be any different?'

She reached out to touch him, but Chip shrank away. 'I'm old enough to do what I like.'

'And what's that? Do you want to go with Spindor, or not?'

Chip threw the question back at her. 'Do you?'

'Yes,' she admitted, 'I think I do. Like him, I'll be sorry to leave but I've had enough of moving from place to place; never knowing where I'll sleep, or if there'll be anything to eat. Also, if I stayed in one place for a while I might be able to find a school to go to, before it's too late.'

Chip's face was expressionless. 'In that case, you'd better go with Spindor.'

'Chip!'

But he walked off without looking back and after that, either avoided being alone with her, or ignored her completely.

'I don't know what's got into him,' she confided to Dig.

'Maybe he's jealous.'

Sky laughed. 'Of Spindor and me?'

'No, of course not. Of us.'

During their time on the Tip, Chip had always been very close to Dig. But, ever since the rescue, the two had hardly spent any time together. It was almost as if they had outgrown each other.

'I suppose you could be right, Dig. But you haven't actually said what you're going to do.' Sky held her breath as she waited for his reply.

'I don't think living out of doors is doing me much good. I'm getting stronger and my breathing's improving, but the cold damp nights aren't good and mid-winter could be a killer. So I was thinking of going with Spindor.'

She struggled to hide her disappointment. 'Just for the good of your health?'

'It's not just that. I might get the chance to finish my article too,' he said, having difficulty keeping his face straight.

Sky fell on Dig and pummelled him. 'You beast! You're doing this on purpose!'

'Ow! You know perfectly well I want to be with you.'

'Well, why didn't you say so, instead of making me drag it out of you?'

Dig's face was totally serious when he confessed, 'I wasn't sure if you'd want me to come.'

'Idiot!' She hugged him. 'You know, from now on, I want you with me wherever I go.' As they finished hugging, Sky noticed Chip had been watching. He stalked off. 'Oh, dear.'

'Would you like me to talk to him?'

Sky shook her head. 'No, better leave it. I expect he'll come round in the end.'

Gentle had no doubts about what she wanted to do. From the moment Sky told her she would have the chance to plant her own herb garden with the seeds she collected, Gentle was determined to go with Spindor. But by the time their last day with the troupe arrived, Chip had still not spoken to Sky.

Sky went through her final performance with very mixed feelings. She had never been entirely comfortable appearing in front of an audience, but she knew she would miss the troupe. When Sky came off, she happily handed over all her tricks to Supermouse. Chip, who had been watching her, turned and stalked off up the hill behind the camp.

A small farewell party had been arranged but, because everyone was sad to be losing people, it was a muted affair and Chip did not turn up for it.

'I'm really worried about him,' she told Dig.

As everyone began to settle down for the night, Dig launched into one of his long, haunting melodies on the pipes. Sky decided she must go and find Chip.

Dig offered to go too, but she refused. 'This is something I've got to do alone.'

With Dig's music soaring in the air around her, Sky clambered up the hill. She paused at the top, looking out across the moonlit landscape, at the dots of light coming from the scattering of shadowy houses. Way off in the distance, there was an orange glow coming from quite a big fire. Sky shivered as she wondered if that was the work of Skulls.

Chip was not difficult to find. He was sitting just below her, on the slope, staring at the moon.

Not wanting to scare him off, Sky was still some distance away when she said, 'Chip, why are you sitting out here, all on your own?'

He mumbled, 'With you and everyone leaving tomorrow, I thought I'd better get used to being on my own.'

As Sky got closer, she realised Chip was crying. 'Oh, Chip! You know you can come with us if you want to.'

'That's the trouble,' he snuffled. 'I don't know what I want. I want to stay with Suds and Flipper, but I don't want to lose you and Dig. I've already lost Mum and Dad. If I lose you I won't have anyone.'

Sky started slightly. Not only could she not remember when Chip had last mentioned their parents, but she suddenly realised she was no longer having any dreams about her mother and she knew there was something deeply sad about both those facts.

Slowly she became aware of the faint sound of Dig's music and it seemed as if the notes were curling about her and caressing her skin. Carefully, Sky slipped an arm round Chip's shoulder and, although he resisted at first, she drew him towards her. 'Chip, you're not losing me. You can come with me.'

Chip sobbed, 'But you don't need me any more.'

'Of course I do!'

'No, you don't. You've got Dig.'

'So have you.'

'But that's not the same, is it?' Chip wailed.

'No,' Sky admitted, 'it isn't. But, whatever happens, I'll always be there for you. Dig, Spindor and Gentle too. Look, Chip, if you aren't sure what you want, why don't you stay with Suds and Flipper for a while? See how you feel and then, if you change your mind and you want to come to Spindor's, you can.'

Chip cautiously asked, 'Are you sure you won't mind?'

'Of course I'll mind! But it's your life.'

'Oh, Sky, I thought you were going to get mad at me and make me go with you.'

'Is that what all this has been about?'

Chip wiped his eyes on the sleeves of his jumper and nodded.

'You should have said. Well, I'll miss you like crazy and be glad when the bad weather comes, so that I get to see you again, but you're old enough to make up your own mind. Come on, let's go back to the others.'

'You go, I'll be along in a minute.'

Just as Sky reached the brow of the hill, drawn by Dig's music, she paused and turned back. Looking down at the tiny figure of Chip, hunched up, all alone in the moonlight, she whispered to herself, 'Oh, I will miss you, Chip. You don't know how much!'

'Are you all ready?' Spindor asked.

Gentle, Dig and Sky all nodded.

It was early in the morning, the sun was shining brightly, but there were troughs of thick morning mist hanging on in the valleys. Only Suds and Chip had woken up in time to see them off, the others having said their goodbyes during the party.

'Then I think we ought to make a start,' Spindor said.

Everybody hugged, and the longest was a three-part hug between Sky, Chip and Dig.

As they reluctantly drew apart, Sky asked Chip, 'You're quite sure you don't want to change your mind?'

There was only a brief pause, before Chip shook his head. 'No, I'm staying. At least for a while.'

Dig slapped him on the back. 'Take care.'

'Sure,' Chip said, looking down at the earth he was stirring round with his foot, 'and you look out for Sky.'

Putting his arm round Sky's shoulder, Dig replied, 'I'll do my best.'

Spindor climbed into the front of the pick-up, 'Come on, we've got a long drive ahead of us!'

He had not mentioned it to anyone, but his eye was on a bunch of Skulls he had spotted some distance off. They had emerged from the mist and then stayed perfectly still, silhouetted against the skyline, watching him. Determined though Spindor was not to run any more, he was not looking for trouble and was anxious to be off.

Dig helped Gentle and Sky up into the back. As they drove away, with the waving figures of Suds and Chip getting ever smaller, Sky reached out to Dig. 'Everything's going to be all right, isn't it?'

Giving her a lopsided grin, Dig took hold of Sky's hand and gave it a big squeeze. 'Got to be, hasn't it?' He took out his pipes and played happy music to try and cheer her up.

But, in her head, Sky could only hear the long, lilting lament which he had played the previous night, while she was sitting in the moonlight, on the hillside, with Chip.